Sworn Statement by William J. Webb

Mr Davies asked me to write this for his book, he said no one would believe a word of it if I didn't. Well, it is true, and I don't care if you believe it or not. Of course, it's not quite the same as when I told it to him. When I read the book it made me laugh, but it didn't seem all that funny at the time. More sort of strange. And all those feelings and thoughts he says I was having just before the end ... well, I don't know about that. Mostly I was just scared, as a matter of fact.

I don't know whether I'm glad or sorry that I met Alfonso Bonzo, but I do know that I'm glad it's all over now.

Billy Webb

Billy Webb
Splott Street
Coventry

PS – I have almost given up swapping things now.

Author's Note

This is a true story, but you don't have to believe it if you don't want to. It's about some strange and funny things that happened to a boy called Billy Webb. He told me the story last year when we were both in hospital (I was under observation for suspected brainrot and he had a broken leg). I was a bit woozy at the time, so I may have got some of the details wrong, but when he told it, I thought it was one of the best stories I had ever heard, weird, funny, and a bit frightening towards the end. So when the brainrot cleared up, I decided to write it all down in a book, and here it is. Reading this book may well be the most useful thing you will ever do, because one day you might meet Alfonso Bonzo too. Recent reports indicate that he is still around.

Contents

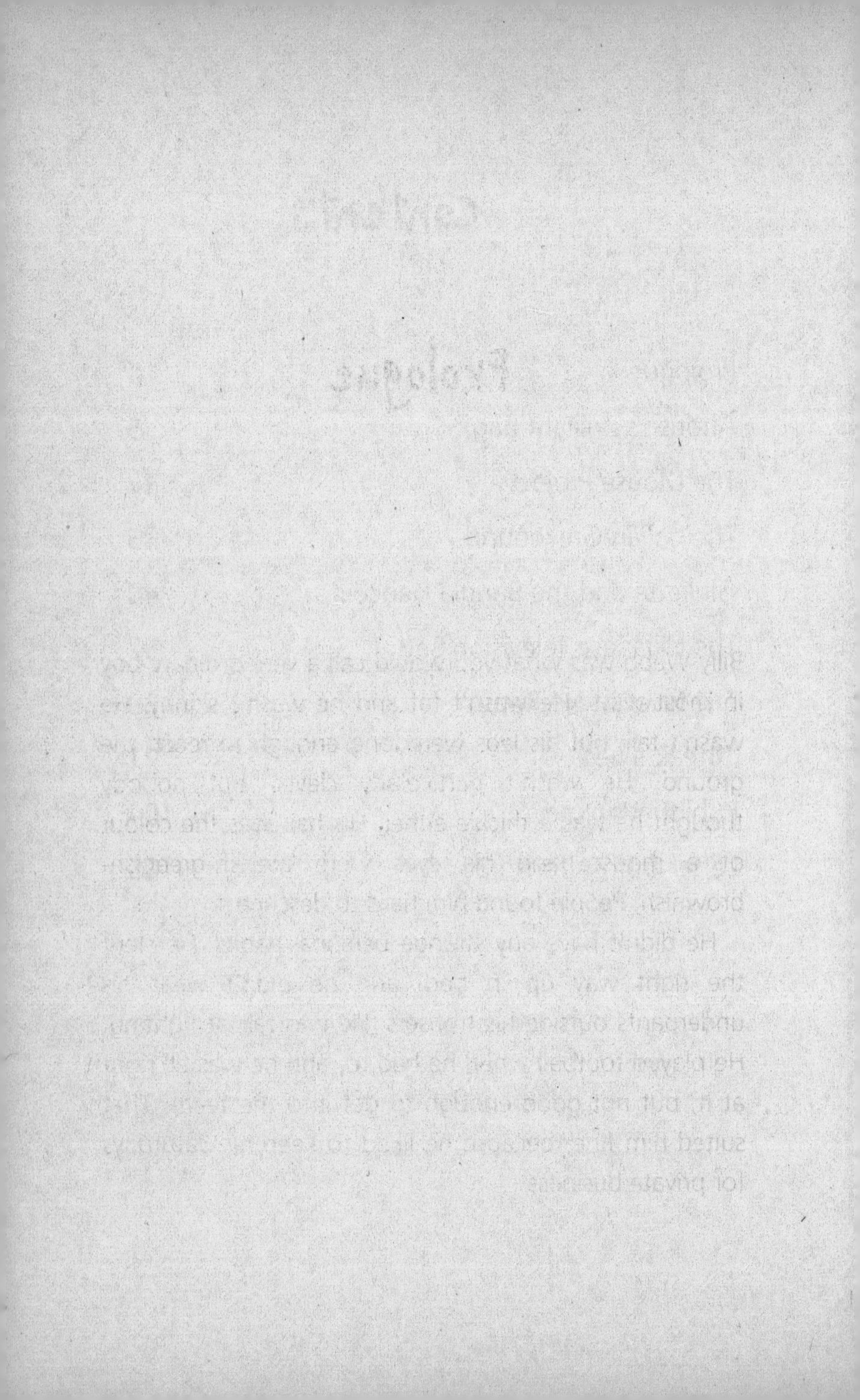

Prologue

Billy Webb was what you would call a very ordinary boy in most ways. He wasn't fat and he wasn't skinny. He wasn't tall, but his legs were long enough to reach the ground. He wasn't particularly clever, but nobody thought he was a thickie either. His hair was the colour of a mouse, and his eyes were greyish-greenish-brownish. People found him hard to describe.

He didn't have any strange personal habits. He slept the right way up in bed, and he didn't wear his underpants outside his trousers. He was fair at fighting. He played football when he had to, and he was all right at it, but not good enough to get into the team. That suited him fine, because he liked to keep his Saturdays for private business.

At school, he tended to melt into the background. He kept his nose clean and his head down and a low profile. He mucked about a bit in art and food technology like most people, but he wasn't famous for it. He sat at the back and he was good at looking busy when he wasn't. He never volunteered for anything. In fact, apart from Mrs Peasgood, his class teacher, most of the teachers had trouble remembering who he was. His school reports said: "Average".

But in one respect Billy Webb was not average: he was exceptional; and that was in his passion for swapping things. He would swap all the usual sorts of things that everyone swaps, such as marbles, autographs, and books, but also more unusual things like white mice, tropical fish, and false moustaches. He would swap for lendsies or for keepsies, for five minutes, a day, a week, or for ever. He never liked to let a day go by without swapping something, and he always went to school with his pockets and his school bag full of possible swapping items. This made him a useful and popular boy at school. Whenever anyone found they'd got something the wrong size or the wrong colour, or two aunties had given them the same thing for Christmas, they'd think: "Never mind. I bet I can do a swap with Billy Webb." And they would usually be right.

He didn't know why it made him feel so good to walk home everyday with his hand in his pocket, feeling the warm nubbly surface of a newly swapped penknife, or the solid sweaty bulge of a genuine American baseball. It wasn't that he particularly loved the penknife or the baseball for themselves: it was more that they were both really good swaps, and they made life exciting, full of change and possibilities. He would often take something in exchange that he didn't really want, just for the sake of a good swap. For instance, sitting on his bedroom shelf was a beautiful model sailing boat. It had been there for four weeks, since he had swapped it with Raymond Fox for a set of pram wheels and axles. Billy was not in the least interested in sailing boats, but he knew that sooner or later someone would turn up who was, and then he'd really be in business.

His mother and father didn't object to his hobby. It didn't cost any money and it kept him out of mischief, they thought. On just one occasion he had got into bad trouble with his mum, and that was when he swapped the new pullover she'd knitted him for three old Elvis LPs. Billy had to go out again and swap the Elvis records for a denim jacket with real imitation sheepskin lining, only two sizes too big, but she still wasn't satisfied.

"I didn't spend two months on that pullover to see it walking up the street on Scott Barnacle!" she said. "You go out again and get it off him. Let him go home to his mother looking like the Lone Ranger's poor relation!"

Billy didn't really mind. And he didn't do anything as simple as going straight to Scott Barnacle. He knew the denim jacket was a really good swap. He took it down to Nigel Creamer's house, and Nigel Creamer's big brother gave him four pool cues and a set of miniature snooker balls for it. Then he went round to Scott Barnacle's and got his pullover back for two of the cues and the snooker balls, keeping the other two cues for spare swaps.

Billy Webb never boasted about his one talent, but privately he thought that he just might be the best swapper in the world.

That was before he met Alfonso Bonzo.

Alfonso's Brilliant Bag

That Monday morning Billy was, as usual, awake before anyone else in the house. He liked the feeling of being awake while everyone else in the house was asleep. He liked listening to them snoring in their different ways: Linda sounding as if she had a taxi ticking over in the back bedroom, Mum making little whimpery growls that were so unlike her bold daylight self, and Dad's random pig-like snorts building up to a climax that sounded like a big duck belching. None of them knew what they sounded like when they were asleep, but Billy did, and that was a good feeling.

Another thing about waking up early was that it was a good time to get some thinking done, before your brain went foggy and damp like the weather outside.

There was always a chance in the early morning that the day might turn out to be weird and different, before all the people got up and started clomping into their routines and making it just the same as yesterday. Also, Billy had the feeling that there were more good ideas floating around for the taking while the morning was still fresh and quiet, and if there were, he would get first crack at them.

Billy needed some good ideas. He needed them for his project. His project was about mice, and it was due to be handed in that morning. It was supposed to be about ten pages long, full of drawings and graphs and bits copied out of reference books, but made to look as if they were in your own words. Billy's project was not like that. After he had written about half a page and done a not very good drawing of a mouse in a trap, he had realized a) that he didn't know as much about mice as he had thought, but b) he knew quite as much about mice as he wanted to, and c) a funny thing about projects was that they made you less interested in things, not more.

It was no good. The mouse project was doomed. Billy did not believe in fighting doom. If you left it alone, doom could sometimes switch sides, and arrange a fire drill or a hymn practice or a lucky rash of spots to get you off the hook. Anyway, when you've had three thoughts like a, b, and c, part of your brain seems to close down for a short holiday. Yes, the mice were going to have to look after themselves. Billy switched over to a part of his brain that was always active, and started to think about the day's swaps. Then he heard the whistling, stopped thinking, and listened.

The first thing about the whistling was that it was definitely not any of the regular early morning whistlers, like the milkman or the postman. The second thing was that it was a really flashy performance, whole songs with all the twiddly bits included and every note clear, pure and melodious, not a bit like ordinary absent-minded whistling. The third thing about the whistling was that it started at the far end of the street, came gradually closer, and stopped just under Billy's window. Then there was a soft knock on the front door.

Billy got out of bed and looked out of the window. His bedroom was the little one just over the front door, and when he looked down all he could see was the top of a broad-brimmed hat made of light green suede. Then a brown hand with two gold rings came out from under the hat and tapped lightly on the door again.

Billy went downstairs and opened the door. On the pavement stood a tall young man with a suntanned face, bright blue eyes and long brown curly hair cascading down from his big green hat. He wore a dazzling white T-shirt, and over it an embroidered jacket with pictures of jungles and monkeys on it. One leg of his trousers was yellow and the other was green, and he carried a dark red leather bag slung over his shoulder .

"E arrivato Alfonso!" said the young man.

"What?" said Billy suspiciously.

The young man smiled. It was an amazing smile, the sort that most people never get smiled at with in a lifetime. It was as bright and full of possibilities as a new comic, and it smelt of chocolate ice cream .

"Scusi," said the young man. "I introduce proper. I am Alfonso Bonzo, Italian Exchange Student." And he gave a little bow. To his surprise and embarrassment Billy found himself bowing back. This was daft. What was he doing, standing on the doorstep at seven in the morning in his stripy pyjamas, bowing to a mad foreign hippy?

"Pleased to meet," said Alfonso Bonzo, and gave another big smile. This one was like a hand-built racing bike and smelt of lavender.

"Look," said Billy. "My dad's not up yet."

"I don't want no pappa," said Alfonso Bonzo.

"Nor's my mum, nor my sister," said Billy.

"No mama, no sister, not today thank you," said Alfonso Bonzo "I come to see you, Billy Webb, because I think maybe you are just the boy for me."

"How d'you mean?" said Billy. He was starting to feel a bit uneasy. Maybe Alfonso Bonzo was an Italian kidnapper, and he'd be snatched off his own doorstep and held to ransom for his dad's beer-mat collection. He took a step backwards.

"Not to worry," said Alfonso Bonzo "I just come for a little exchange. Alfonso Bonzo, Italian exchange student. I exchange things, capisci?"

"Oh," said Billy. "You mean like swaps."

"Si, si, like swaps, exactamente, you one clever boy, you catch on quick."

"What do you swap?" said Billy.

"Anything," said Alfonso Bonzo.

"So do I," said Billy.

"So how you like to make a little exchange with Alfonso Bonzo?"

"I might," said Billy, cautiously. "What have you got?"

"How you like this bag?" Billy looked at the bag properly for the first time. It was made of a wonderfully rich dark red leather, you could tell it was real leather from the warm scenty smell; and it was embossed all over with a design of monkeys climbing trees and swinging from each other's tails. It had a long strap made of the same leather, and a clasp that looked like real gold, in the shape of two intertwined monkey's paws. It wasn't Billy

Webb's sort of bag, but it was quite definitely a Really Good Swap.

"Not bad," said Billy. (A good swapper never seems too keen.) "What do you want for it?"

"Straight-a swapping down the line, a bag for a bag, that's the way Alfonso like to do exchanges," said Alfonso Bonzo. "You got a little bag for me,?"

"Only my school bag," said Billy. "Sorry."

"Bring him out then, let's have a look at him, I think maybe we have a nice exchange here!"

You won't say that when you see it, thought Billy, as he ran up the stairs quietly in his bare feet. Everything was normal upstairs: taxi throbbing in the back room, whimpering, wheezing and quacking from the big front bedroom. Billy got his bag and took it downstairs, half expecting to find Alfonso Bonzo gone and the pavement empty. But there he was, smiling a smile like a pile of presents under a Christmas tree, and he held out his hand for Billy's school bag.

"Good sort of bag, that," said Billy, trying to make the best of it. But it wasn't a good sort of bag. From anybody's point of view it was a bad sort of bag. It was made of frayed blue nylon with cracked plastic edging and buckles, one of which was broken. There were several dodgy-looking stains, and a hole where his compass poked through. On the back it said "Billy

Webb" in not very neat red ballpoint, and next to that was the biggest of the dodgy-looking stains, where Scott Barnacle had written "is a prat" and Billy had tried to rub it out. It was not a good bag and it was not a good swap.

"OK," said Alfonso Bonzo "I make you small exchange." Billy couldn't believe his luck, but he kept his head.

"Lendsies, or keepsies?" he said.

"Trial offer, one day exchange, I think we both have lovely times with strange new bags. Tomorrow, same time, Alfonso Bonzo come back to you, we swap back, maybe talk another little exchange, OK?"

"OK then," said Billy, starting to take his school things out of the bag.

"Hey, what you doing here?" said Alfonso "All that stuff belong to Alfonso Bonzo for today. I get your stuff, you get mine, nice surprise for Bonzo, nice surprise for Billy Webb, I think you like it. Otherwise, no deal, and you don't see Alfonso Bonzo any more. Think it over."

Billy thought it over for about five seconds.

"OK," he said. "It's a swap." Alfonso Bonzo swung Billy's schoolbag jauntily over his shoulder.

"I don't think you regret," he said. "Arrivederci, Billy Webb, you one very nice boy for business, I think we make a good exchange today!"

* * *

A bit later on that morning, Billy Webb was beginning to wonder if he had made such a good exchange. About five minutes after Alfonso Bonzo had gone whistling off down the street, Billy had remembered that his mouse project was one of the things in the bag. It wasn't much of a project, but it was all he had, and he couldn't quite see himself explaining to Mrs Peasgood about Alfonso Bonzo. The next disappointment was that try as he might, by force or cunning, he couldn't get the monkey's hand clasp on the red leather bag to open. He wrestled with it so long that it made him late for breakfast; and after breakfast he had a lot of trouble stuffing it under his coat. (He didn't fancy explaining to his mum about Alfonso Bonzo either.) And as he walked down Splott Street on the way to school, looking like a boy who had just eaten a whole packet of cornflakes without taking them out of the box first, it suddenly occurred to him that Alfonso Bonzo's bag was not such a good swap after all because he couldn't swap it. He was stuck with it until seven o'clock tomorrow morning.

By the time he reached the school gate people were beginning to point at him and make witty remarks about square bellies and boys with their bottoms on back to front. Billy, who hated being the centre of attention, decided that nothing could be worse than this. Trying to look casual and absent-minded about it, he unzipped his coat and slung the dark red leather bag over his shoulder.

It was a mistake. Now *everyone* was looking at him. It seemed as if all the skipping and the football and the chasing and the shouting had stopped all at once, and the whole school was standing still staring at him. It was as bad as one of those dreams when you go to school dressed in your pyjamas. And just as if it were a dream, Ginger Gahagan and his friends, the four hardest boys in the whole school, who had been practising head-butts on each other by the railings, turned slowly and sauntered towards Billy Webb with evil grins slowly forming on their faces .

Ginger Gahagan stopped in front of Billy and grinned down at him. Ginger Gahagan was big. He had big red hands, and big feet in big black Doc Marten boots, and a big head that was all shiny and lumpy at the front, like a caveman's club, from all the butting and nutting he had done. Everything about Ginger Gahagan was big except for his eyes, which were small, green and crusty, and set so close together that they seemed to be growing in his nose.

"You're a girlie-girl," said Ginger Gahagan.

"No I'm not," said Billy.

"You're a girlie-girl. You got a girl's bag."

"Good bag this," said Billy. "Bet you wish you had one like it." He meant this to sound strong and determined, but it came out as a strangled mutter.

"Give it here then, girlie." Ginger Gahagan held out his hand for it.

Billy didn't move or speak.

"Just for lends," said Ginger Gahagan, grinning. Billy held on tight to the bag and took a step backwards. Ginger Gahagan never gave back lends. He would either keep the bag, or sell it, or stomp it to tatters. Billy was beginning to hate the bag and wish he'd never seen it, but he knew he was going to have to try to protect it for a whole day. He longed for the bell to go. Their school didn't have a nice punctual electric bell like everyone else; instead, he had to wait for old Mr Potter and his hand bell. He imagined Potter shuffling along the corridor, whistling between his teeth, holding the bell in his freckly old hands, fingers closed firmly over the clapper, coming out on to the steps, looking at his watch, any second now it would go...

"Let's get him," said Wayne Ratkin.

Billy went into a panic. He jumped back, unslung Affonso Bonzo's bag from his shoulder, and started to whirl it round his head. It was a hopeless weapon. It felt light and flimsy and awkward to swing, but it might hold them off for a second or two. Wayne Ratkin and

Messer Bullwinkel hesitated, but Ginger Gahagan came right ahead, and Billy resigned himself to his fate.

Then something strange happened. Everything seemed to go into slow motion. The cold flutter in Billy's stomach went away. He felt warm, solid, even cheerful. And Alfonso Bonzo's bag was getting heavier and heavier, but somehow easier and easier to handle, whistling slowly round his head like a planet in the solar system. Billy saw Ginger Gahagan lunge forward and make a grab for the strap, but he seemed to be moving as slowly and clumsily as a man under water. Billy leaned back gently, like a matador. He seemed to have all the time in the world. Ginger's fingers missed the strap, and he stumbled forward, off balance. Billy wasn't aware of aiming the bag. He just let it swing round again on its own momentum, and it thunked into Ginger Gahagan's midriff. There was a great pungent whoosh as all the smelly breath in Ginger Gahagan's body shot out of his mouth, and he sat down on the playground, his crusty little green eyes staring at Billy in amazement and fear.

"Hit him again, Billy," advised Scott Barnacle. But Billy didn't feel like it. He hadn't wanted any trouble in the first place; he just wanted to be left alone. And in a strange way he felt sorry for Ginger Gahagan. He had always thought of him as a bit of a monster, but now he looked puffy, pathetic and bewildered as he sat there on the damp concrete gasping for breath. Billy felt the strength and the warm solid feeling drain out of him. The bag felt lighter too, and hung limply from his shoulder. How could he have knocked Ginger Gahagan down with it?

After a few minutes Ginger Gahagan got his breath back and said, "I'll get you for this, Billy Webb." But he didn't make any move towards doing so, he didn't even get up, and nobody believed him. Then all the kids in Billy's class clustered round him, telling him what a great fighter he was and asking for a feel of his brilliant fighting bag. Billy was a hero for the first time in his life, and he didn't like it. Being a hero made his face feel hot and his legs feel numb and his brains feel scrambled. Being a hero was almost as bad as being a girl.

Then, after what seemed like several hours but was actually about a minute and a half, old Potter finally got his act together, wheezed out on to the steps, and rang the bell.

The Mouse Project

It was a relief to be in the classroom. Billy's place was at the back, in the far corner from Mrs Peagood's table, right out of the limelight. He slid Alfonso Bonzo's bag under the table where no one could see it, and he got his head down over his reading book so that no one could see him either. If he angled his position carefully even Mrs Peasgood couldn't see him, because Pritti Shah, who sat in front of him, always sat up straight, to make up for being small and thin. Another useful thing about Pritti Shah was that everything about her was pretty, not just her name. She had very big dark brown eyes for the size of her face, a small straight brown nose that never went red or runny, and she smiled a lot in a shy sort of way. She also wore very bright clothes in colours like orange, purple and green. The result of this was that very few teachers looked at Billy Webb when they could be looking at Pritti Shah, even Mrs Peasgood.

Mrs Peasgood finished the register, then went to the blackboard and started writing up the day's routine. Billy crossed his fingers and squeezed Alfonso's bag between his knees. Maths, two pages minimum, Literacy Hour, finishing the follow-up to Friday's TV programme . . . it was going to be all right. She had forgotten about Billy's mice. He could get through the day (hopefully without any more bag trouble), get his own bag back first thing tomorrow, and maybe even finish his project. Why not? Such a lot of odd things had happened already today that he was beginning to think that anything was possible. Then Pritti Shah turned round and beamed her huge brown eyes at him at point blank range .

"Hey, Billy," she said. "That was good when you knocked Ginger Gahagan down." Billy felt himself going red in the face again.

"I hate him," said Pritti. "He hits my brother every day."

"He hits everyone," muttered Billy. He liked Pritti Shah, but he wished she'd turn round and ignore him like she usually did.

"I think your new bag is brilliant," said Pritti. "Can I have a look at it?"

"Pritti Shah, I'd like to see your face, not your back," said Mrs Peasgood suddenly. Pritti turned round and Billy put his head down so quickly that he banged his nose on his reading book. But he was too late.

"Ah, yes, Billy Webb!" said Mrs Peasgood. "We nearly forgot your project, didn't we?" Billy lifted his nose out of *The Mouse and His Child* (he had thought the book might be useful for the project but it had no proper facts in it and the Mouse himself had turned out to be clockwork) and stared miserably at Mrs Peasgood.

"No time like the present," said Mrs Peasgood. "Let's have an oral presentation, shall we?"

An oral presentation meant you had to stand up in front of the class and talk about it, and then answer questions. Mrs Peasbody was keen on oral presentations. She said they helped you with Life Skills, whatever they were. Billy Webb hated oral presentations because they made his mouth go dry and his ears buzz, and all his friends could have a good laugh at him. Oral presentations were dreadful, and this one was double dreadful because he didn't have anything to orally present.

"Can I do it tomorrow?" he asked hopelessly.

"No," said Mrs Peasgood firmly.

Billy stood up feeling like a condemned prisoner. Then suddenly a thought flashed into his head. Alfonso's bag wouldn't open! He'd take it up to Mrs Peasgood's table, fiddle with the clasp, Mrs Peasgood would fiddle, Nigel Creamer the technological wizard would fiddle, but it wouldn't open and the oral presentation would have to be postponed. Brilliant!

Billy picked up the bag and strode to Mrs Peasgood's table.

"Gather round, children," said Mrs Peasgood. Billy banged the red leather bag on the table, and fiddled with the monkey's paw clasp. To his horror, it opened immediately, and a dark red ring-bound file slid out of it on to the table. Billy looked down at it, startled. On the front in gold letters were the words: MOUSE PROJECT. His hands were shaking a bit and his fingers felt as fat and clumsy as bananas as he opened the file to the first page. It was empty. So was the next page. So were all the pages after that. Slowly he looked up from the file at Mrs Peasgood. His mouth was dry and his ears were buzzing.

"Don't be nervous, Billy," said Mrs Peasgood. "Just tell us a bit about it in your own words first, don't read it out."

Billy opened and closed his mouth but no words came out. This was not surprising, because there were no thoughts in his mind, just a huge roaring blur of embarrassment. Out of the corner of his eye he saw Nigel Creamer whisper something to Raymond Fox, and Raymond Fox started to laugh. Soon they would all be laughing at him. Maybe he could play for time and there would be a fire drill, or Darnell Masuda might have one of his fits. He cleared his throat lengthily, undid the top button of his shirt and did it up again. That took about four seconds, during which the fire bell remained obstinately silent, and Darnell Masuda, far from falling off his chair and rolling on the floor, grinned cheerfully at Billy and flicked a nosepicking at him.

"Tell us how you first got interested in mice, Billy," said Mrs Peasgood in a wearily patient sort of voice.

"Well," said Billy. His voice was back! Maybe he could just sort of make it up as he went along.

"I first got interested in mice when I got a pair of white mice in a swap with this kid called Brett Icing, he goes to Shortlands."

"Brett Icing? What sort of stupid name is that?" said Scott Barnacle.

"You can talk," said Billy, who was quite glad of the interruption. "Scott Barnacle! If you ask me, that's just as stupid a name as Brett Icing!"

"Miss, miss, he's not called Brett Icing!" squealed Annette Osoba, bouncing up and down on her chair with her hand up. "I know him, and he's called Brett Icerink!"

"No, he's not," said Billy. "Nobody's called Icerink."

"Well Brett Icerink is 'cos I know his cousin, right?" said Annette Osoba fiercely.

"I know a girl called Annette Kirton," said Raymond Fox.

"I know a girl called Lydia Dustbin!" yelled Jason Epstein.

"Right!" said Mrs Peasgood when everyone had stopped laughing. "That's enough about names. Get on with the story, Billy."

"Can I say what the mice were called?" asked Billy.

Mrs Peasgood narrowed her eyes and gave him one of her looks. "All right," she said.

"I called them Whitey and Snowy," said Billy.

"Not very original," said Mrs Peasgood.

"What would you have called them, then, Miss?"

"All right, all right! Carry on!" said Mrs Peasgood. "No more interruptions. Even from me."

So Billy told the class the sad but true story of his short career as a mouse breeder. Whitey and Snowy settled down happily in an old rabbit hutch, got married, and started breeding. Billy had been able to sell, give away or swap most of the babies, keeping a few back for more breeding. Before long nearly everyone he knew had one or two white mice from Webb's Mouse Farm, as he had come to call it. Billy had to expand his premises, swapping white mice for new hutches, selling white mice to buy the food for the new mice to eat. He was beginning to wonder if he was turning into a mouse millionaire. He was spending all his time with the mice now, pairing them, separating new families, feeding them, mucking out, finding new clients for swaps and sales. The garden shed where he kept his basic stock of ordinary swapping mice, and his bedroom where the classy breeders lived, were both full of the smell of mice and the scuttling and scampering of their little twiggy legs, and the whirring of the wheels they exercised on.

Billy knew he was telling the story well. The whole class was quiet. Raymond Fox and Scott Barnacle had stopped playing noughts and crosses, and Annette Osoba was so intent that she was sucking her big toe without noticing what she was doing. But what was bothering Billy was the odd whirring sound, a bit like the whirring of a mouse-wheel, but more like the whirring and pattering of a distant fax machine like the one he'd seen in the building society office. And it seemed to be coming from Alfonso Bonzo's red leather file. Billy paused in the story, and the whirring and pattering stopped. Funny. It must be in his head. Maybe he was going to have a fit.

"Carry on, Billy," said Mrs Peasgood. "You're doing fine."

Billy started talking again, and the whirring and pattering started up again too. He told them how the mouse farm reached a crisis. Everyone he knew had at least one of his white mice, and they were still breeding. He had flooded the market. Then Theophilus entered the scene. (Whirrbrrrrr patter patter.) Theophilus was a wild brown warehouse mouse, who had climbed into Billy's dad's bag, and instead of killing him Billy's dad had brought him home. Billy decided that he would try to breed a new sort of mouse that no one had seen before, so that demand would rise again. He was a bit worried about putting Theophilus in with the tame white mice. Theophilus was smaller than them, and there was only one of him, and Billy was worried that he might get beaten up; but on the other hand Theophilus looked tough and mean, like a mouse who knew how to look after himself in a tight corner, so Billy decided to give it a go and put Theophilus in the main mouse hutch.

When he came down in the morning, he found a gruesome scene in the main mouse hutch. Theophilus had killed all the male white mice. He was sitting by the pile of bodies, looking up at Billy in a mean and self-satisfied way, while the female white mice huddled in a corner gazing at Theophilus, the killer of their husbands and brothers, with what looked like great affection and admiration.

"Billy Webb," said Mrs Peasgood. "This project of yours is beginning to sound a bit sexist."

"Not my fault, Miss," said Billy. "Theophilus was a sexist. And a fightist.

"All right," said Mrs Peasgood. "Carry on."

And Billy told the rest of the terrible story of the downfall of Webb's Mouse Farm: how Theophilus's children had all taken after Theophilus, except that they were much bigger; how he had been unable to sell or swap any of them because they were so fierce and ugly. How, after killing off all the remaining white mice, they had taken to fighting amongst themselves (whirr whirr patter patter thunk!) and how finally one night they had chewed through the wire netting and escaped, causing the great mouse plague of Splott Street, which had taken the Council Ratman three weeks to clear up; and how Billy's mum had told him she never wanted to see a mouse again.

"And that's how I got interested in mice," said Billy.

"Fine," said Mrs Peasgood. "Give him a clap."

Billy got such a big round of applause that he started to get embarrassed again. He put his head down and started fiddling with the red leather file to give his hands something to do. As he turned over the first page he saw something that made him gasp with amazement. It was covered with handwriting, his own handwriting, except it was much neater than usual and with more capital letters and full stops. It was a beautifully written version of the story he had just told, and it went on for five pages, with brilliant pencil drawings of Whitey, Snowy, and Theophilus, and a diagram of how to lay out a breeding hutch. He shut the file quickly and looked up at Mrs Peasgood again, feeling dazed and shaky.

"Can I sit down now, Miss?"

"Not yet," said Mrs Peasgood. "Tell us a bit about how you went on from there."

"Well, um. . ." said Billy. Of course he hadn't gone on anywhere from there. But Mrs Peasgood wouldn't be satisfied with that. From the direction of the file he could hear a faint humming. He racked his brains.

"I thought I might start with a sort of diagram family tree sort of thing, about how the mice got bred." Before he had finished the sentence, the humming changed to the now familiar whirring and pattering. Billy glanced down at the file, and up again guiltily at Mrs Peasgood, but no one except himself seemed to be able to hear the sound. After three or four seconds it stopped.

"And?" said Mrs Peasgood.

Holding his breath, Billy opened the file again. Inside it was a folded sheet of graph paper. Billy opened it. It was enormous. At the top it said:

WEBB'S MOUSE FARM: BREEDING RECORD

It started at the top with Whitey and Snowy, then opened up into a huge family tree showing every mouse that had been born and what had happened to it.

Theophilus appeared about halfway down, and all the deaths and escapes were shown in red and green crosses. Wordlessly, Billy held it up so that everyone could see it. They stared at it in dead silence. Even Mrs Peasgood's jaw hung open.

And suddenly, Billy stopped feeling shaky and dazed, as he suddenly realized that he was in control of the situation. He didn't know what was happening or why, but whatever it was, he was in charge of it.

"Anyway," he said. "What I really wanted to do was find out about training mice, how they learn and that." The whirring and pattering started again, but this time it came from the bag, not from the file. It stopped with a click, and Billy opened the bag, and felt inside. His brain didn't know what he was feeling for, but his fingers did: a long rectangular box with little metal bars down the side. He took it out and put it on the table.

"Miss!" squealed Claire Preedy. "He's got real mice in there!"

"Don't be silly, Claire," said Mrs Peasgood in a dazed sort of way. "He would, wouldn't he? It's a mouse project after all. Carry on, Billy."

The cage was divided into four compartments, and in each compartment sat a brown and white mouse, sniffing the air and blinking in the light. Billy had no idea what was going to happen, but something whirring and pattering in his brain told him what to say

"This is the science bit of my project," said Billy. "See these four mice? Well, the mouse on the right-hand end is a trained mouse. We'll call him Mouse A. The others are Mouse B, Mouse C and Mouse D. They're all hungry, but Mouse A is the only one who's a trained food hunter. You can probably see that he's already working out what to do."

"Get out of it! They're all the same!" yelled Raymond

"Look harder," said Billy. They looked harder. It was true. All the other mice were just darting about vaguely, but Mouse A was turning his head slowly this way and that, with a keen intelligent expression on his whiskery face.

"Now," said Billy. "I want everyone to keep quiet and sit still for this experiment. I'm going to let the mice out, so that you can see the different ways they behave. Is that all right, Miss?"

"We'll try very hard," said Mrs Peasgood. Billy unhooked the catches on the four compartments. Mouse B came out and wandered round in circles, Mouse C stared intently at Mrs Peasgood and sat down for a scratch, and Mouse D looked round in a frightened sort of way then scuttled to the back of his cage. But Mouse A ran down the leg of the table like a brown and white streak and scampered straight towards Raymond

Fox. Children were squealing and scrambling to get their feet off the floor but Mouse A took no notice. He ran up Raymond Fox's chair leg, up the inside of his sleeve, out again at the collar, then dived into his bag. In two seconds he was out again, carrying a small lump of cheese in his mouth, and racing back for the cage. Billy rattled the metal bars and all the mice went into their compartments. Billy shut the door of the cage and slid it back into Alfonso Bonzo's bag.

"Mouse A wins," he said. "Now the question is, if we breed from mice A, B, C and D, would Mouse A's children be ace food hunters like their father, or would they need to be trained up like Mouse A was? We have seen how Theophilus's family were all fightists and sexists just like he was. Is being a clever food hunter the same sort of thing, or is it something different? And how would you set up an experiment to prove it one way or the other?"

He looked around the class. Kids were looking thoughtful and even scratching their heads. Nigel Creamer put his band up and started bouncing his bottom on the seat and making little strained squeaky noises, rather like the noises Mouse A made, in fact.

"Sir! Sir!" he panted, then went bright. red with embarrassment and put his hand down. But nobody laughed at him. Billy realized that for the past five minutes he had been talking exactly like a teacher; being Firm but Friendly like Mrs Peasgood, and asking a lot of questions he already knew the answers to. This was terrible. In just one morning he had starred as Girl, Hero, and now Teacher, when all he wanted was to be Billy Webb and keep a low profile. And as he thought this, he was aware that the quiet whirring and pattering from inside the bag was slowing down and dying into silence.

"Can I sit down now, Miss?" he asked.

Mrs Peasgood didn't answer for a moment. Her mouth was half open and she looked dazed and puzzled.

For a second, Billy saw what she must have been like when she was a little girl in a classroom about a million years ago.

"Yes, all right," she said eventually. "Thank you, Billy." As he was going back to his seat, the bag clutched firmly under his arm, she spoke again.

"Billy," she said, in a vague sort of way. "Did . . . um . . . I mean did all that actually happen just now?"

"What d'you mean, Miss?" said Billy.

Mrs Peasgood narrowed her eyes and gave him one of her looks. "Literacy," she said. "Numeracy!" she said. "Design and Technology!" she said. "And Darnell Masuda, you can take all the pictures of bare ladies out of your Victorian Pastimes file, because I'll be going through it with you at my table in two minutes, right?"

Mrs Peasgood was herself again.

The rest of the day was strange, or rather, extra normal in a wrong sort of way. Nobody said anything to Billy Webb about the brilliant bag, or the project, or mice A, B, C, or D. It was as if they had all made a secret agreement to ignore the whole business. The classroom was much quieter than usual, and a whole lot of work got done. At break, Billy asked Mrs Peasgood if he could leave the bag in her cupboard for safety. She took it from him without a word, put it in the cupboard, and locked the door. He braced himself for one of her keen searching looks and a lot of awkward and embarrassing questions; but it seemed that she didn't want to meet his eyes any more than he wanted to meet hers.

Sometimes you dream a very vivid dream in which someone you know in real life behaves in a dramatically odd way: say in the dream you go into the bathroom and find the man from the corner shop in your bath playing with your ducks and eating cheese on toast. Even though you know it's a dream, the next time you go in the shop for a Mars bar, it's hard to look him in the eye. He seems to have changed. It was like this with Billy and Mrs Peasgood, and it was like this with Billy and everyone else that day. Everyone treated him in a polite but embarrassed way, as if someone in his family had died, or as if he'd just come out of hospital. And this was fine, and not fine at all, both at the same time.

At home time, Mrs Peasgood unlocked the cupboard, again without a word, and Billy went home with Alfonso Bonzo's bag. Nobody walked with him and nobody called out to him, but out of the corner of his eye he noticed several kids pointing him out in an awed and respectful way. As soon as he was home, he went straight upstairs to his room and shoved Alfonso Bonzo's bag under his bed. He felt better immediately. All in all it hadn't been a bad day at all. He had sorted out Ginger Gahagan, perhaps for ever; and he had sorted out his Mouse Project in a truly spectacular way. All in all Alfonso's bag had been a Really Good Swap. When the mad hippy came back next day, he would swap the bag back for his own ratty old thing, and the Italian Exchange Student would go on his way and out of Billy's life.

Or maybe. Just possibly. Depending on how he felt. He might just consider one more exchange with Alfonso Bonzo.

The Italian Greyhound

A quarter to seven.

The taxi throbbed gently in the back bedroom. Pigs and ducks snorting and quacking in the front bedroom. Billy had been awake and ready since six am, listening for Alfonso Bonzo's melodious whistle. He had made his mind up what he was going to do. He was going to give back the bag, and say no to any more deals. Somehow he felt that Alfonso Bonzo was too big an operator, way out of Billy's class as a swapper (though he would not have admitted this to anyone.) There had been something disturbing about that bag. All that whirring and clicking, for instance. It was as if the bag had contained a powerful computer that hooked up directly to Billy's brain. All very interesting, but he preferred to keep his brain to himself.

At five to seven, Billy couldn't stand it any longer, and went quietly down to the kitchen to see Fred. Fred was the family dog. He was a stocky brown-and-white job of no great beauty, but considerable character. He was absolutely delighted to welcome Billy into his personal chambers so early in the morning. He cavorted about the kitchen, making low moaning sounds from the back of his throat, rather like someone straining on the toilet, and he crashed his warm heavy body repeatedly against Billy's legs, nearly knocking him flat. That was Fred's way of showing affection – he would have no truck with fawning, licking, or any soppiness of that sort. The solid thump of body on body was what Fred liked. Billy liked it too, and found it very comforting just now, because he was feeling just a little bit nervous. He sat down and Fred came over and sat heavily on his feet, his thick tail thumping on the floor. Nothing to worry about. Swap the bags. Cheerio Alfonso. Back to normal .

Then he heard the melodious whistle in the distance. The Cornish Floral Dance with all the fiddly bits it was today. He ran quietly upstairs (throb throb throb snort snort snort QUACK) grabbed the red leather bag from under the bed, ran downstairs again, and opened the front door. Alfonso Bonzo stood on the step with one hand raised ready to knock. Same green hat, same multicoloured jacket, same daft hippy trousers, same brilliant smile. And Billy's old school bag was slung over his shoulder, somehow looking much more elegant than when Billy wore it.

"E arrivato Alfonso," said the Italian Exchange Student.

"Morning," said Billy Webb.

"One lovely day for business, no?"

"Not bad," said Billy, squinting at the sun.

"How you like Alfonso Bonzo's bag?"

"It was OK," said Billy cautiously.

"Hey, you one cool customer, Billy Webb. I bet you have a brilliant time with that bag! Mouse A, Mouse B, no?" (How did he know about Mouse A and Mouse B? Suddenly Billy wanted to get the business over quickly.)

"Maybe I let you keep the bag, and Alfonso keep your bag, souvenir of happy business association." Alfonso Bonzo smiled his racing bike smile, and patted Billy's bag. "Kind of funny, but Alfonso got a lot of time for this ratty old thing!"

"No thanks," said Billy Webb. "Swap back, like we said." The racing bike smile disappeared and Alfonso Bonzo's face clouded over with disappointment, but with something else as well: for a moment he looked almost mean and dangerous. Then the moment went, and the smile came back. Perhaps the mean look had just been a trick of the light.

"OK, Billy Webb. Alfonso is a man of his word." He unslung Billy's bag from his shoulder, and Billy handed him the red leather bag with its gleaming clasp and its coruscations of monkeys. As he did so, he felt a pang of regret. No more Italian exchanges; back to routine.

Behind him he heard the familiar thump-thump-thump along the passage. Fred had come to see what was going on. When Fred saw Alfonso Bonzo, he stood stock still and stared at him in amazement. Then he started a tentative growl at the back of his throat, but stopped halfway through as if having second thoughts.

"Eh, Caro," said the Italian Exchange Student in a low gentle tone, as if he and Fred were old and dear friends meeting after a long separation. Fred put his head down and wiggled his backside, and then, as if embarrassed by this, sat down heavily and started scratching his ear with his back leg.

"Hey, Billy Webb," said Alfonso Bonzo. "That's one very fine dog you got there. What sort of dog you call that dog?"

"Bitzer," said Billy

"Bitzer?"

"You know," said Billy. "Bitzer this, bitzer that." The Italian Exchange Student threw his head back and roared with laughter, as if this were the best joke he had eyer heard.

"You one witty boy," he said. "How you like to make me small exchange with Bitzer?"

"His name's not Bitzer," said Billy. "His name's Fred. And you don't swap dogs."

"Freddo," said Alfonso Bonzo. "Caro Freddo." Fred stopped scratching his ear, wagged his tail, and looked soulfully at Bonzo.

"Just a small exchange," said the Italian. "How you say, lendsies, just like the bags. Freddo don't come to no harm, Alfonso Bonzo treat him like his own brother. Just one day, what do you say? You know Alfonso Bonzo is a man of honour. I know Billy Webb is a boy of honour."

"What have you got to swap?" said Billy. He didn't mean to say it. It just came out.

"Dog for a dog, straight down the line, no messing about, that's how Alfonso like to do business."

"I don't see any dog," said Billy.

Bonzo smiled a smile like the first day of the summer holidays. Then he whistled two low notes and called softly: "Giulietta!"

The little dog must have been waiting just round the corner. One moment it wasn't there, the next it was: a small delicate-looking creature with a supple curvaceous body and slender tapering legs. It was dove grey all over, and wore a little red jacket and a red leather collar with what looked like real diamonds glittering in it. "E arrivata

Giulietta!" said Alfonso Bonzo proudly. Fred got up politely, and the two dogs touched noses and wagged their tails.

"What sort of dog d'you call that?" said Billy.

"Italian greyhound," said Alfonso Bonzo. "Very nice dog, very valuable dog. With this dog, a boy can have one brilliant time!"

"Is she a biter or a fighter?" asked Billy.

"Not a biter, not a fighter. Bit of a dancer, that's all."

"Nice looking little dog," said Billy. Actually, he thought Giulietta was the most beautiful little dog he'd ever seen in his life.

"Giulietta . . . hop-la!" said Alfonso Bonzo softly, and the little greyhound leapt neatly into his arms and snuggled down there, nestling her nose in Bonzo's sleeve.

"Hey, that's good," said Billy.

"You try it, Billy Webb. She do it for me, she do it for you."

Alfonso put Giulietta down on the step .

"Giulietta . . . hop-la!" said Billy, and in an instant his arms were full of warm supple Italian greyhound. He could feel her little heart softly pounding against his chest and her cold nose nuzzling his ear. Giulietta was nothing like what you would call a Billy Webb sort of dog. Far too fancy and delicate, not at all the sort of dog you could keep a low profile with, but Billy was beginning to agree with Alfonso Bonzo He felt sure that a boy could have a brilliant time with a dog like that.

"Well, what do you say, Billy Webb? What do you say, caro Freddo?"

Fred wagged his tail. He looked game for anything.

"Just for a day," said Billy. "Not all night. My dad likes him in at nights."

"Sure," said Alfonso Bonzo "No problem. I get him back to you at half past five, six o'clock, whatever you like."

"OK," said Billy Webb. "You're on."

Giulietta and the Bangla Dancers

"What's this, then, Billy Webb?" asked Mrs Peasgood.

"Italian greyhound, Miss. Good sort of dog, that. Looking after her for a friend."

"Very pretty," said Mrs Peasgood. "You can't bring dogs to school, though, you know that."

"Visual aid, Miss," said Billy hopefully.

"Visual aid?"

"Yes, Miss. Like if you were wanting to do a project on dogs, Miss, or Italy, like. Dead good visual aid, Miss."

Mrs Peasgood started to smile and then gave Billy one of her thoughtful looks.

"You're getting a bit full of yourself these days, Billy Webb," she said.

Billy thought this rather an odd thing to say. Wasn't

everyone full of themselves? If you were only half full of yourself, surely you would sag, wouldn't you? And if you weren't full of yourself, what else would you be full of? Be a bit silly if you were full of somebody else. Wisely, he said none of this to Mrs Peasgood.

"Not trying to be cheeky, Miss," he said. "Just explaining. She'll be dead good and quiet if you let her stay, Miss. She won't muck about, and you can see she's not a biter or a fighter. Brilliant dog, this, Miss."

"What's her name?" asked Mrs Peasgood.

"Giulietta, Miss. Italian name, that is."

"I thought it might be," said Mrs Peasgood.

"On account of her being Italian, Miss."

"I'm not simple minded, Billy."

"Sorry, Miss. Would you like a hold of her? You can have a hold of her for nothing if you like. Mostly I charge."

"That's very generous of you, Billy."

"Thank you, Miss."

Mrs Peasgood looked up. The whole of Class Four were sitting listening to this exchange.

"Nothing to do, folks?" she said in her normal brisk voice. "No reading development cards, no library books, no life-enhancing hobbies? Are we all word-perfect in our parts for assembly? What view do we take of free time in this classroom?"

"Every fleeting moment is pregnant with possibilities," said Class Four as one man and woman .

"Then let me see all those brilliant young noses at the grindstone," said Mrs Peasgood.

She returned her attention to Billy and Giulietta.

"Yes, I would like a hold of her please, Billy."

"What you have to say is 'Giulietta hopla'," said Billy. Mrs Peasgood narrowed her eyes .

"You're not having me on, Billy Webb?"

"No, Miss," said Billy earnestly, and Giulietta wagged her slender long tail and quivered soulfully in expectation.

"Giulietta . . . hopla!" said Mrs Peasgood softly, and Giulietta leapt into her arms and snuggled there. Mrs Peasgood was not what anyone would call a fat teacher, but there was a lot more of her to snuggle into than there was of Billy and his generally bony classmates. Giulietta sighed and closed her eyes .

"Thing is," said Billy after what seemed a suitable pause, 'thing is, Miss, Giulietta's a sensitive dog. Needs company. Couldn't lock her up and leave her at home, could I, Miss?"

"No," agreed Mrs Peasgood. "That'd be awful. OK," she said finally. "God knows, I mean goodness knows what Mr Hardwood's going to say, though. And what about assembly? You're in it, aren't you?"

"She can sit under your chair, Miss," said Billy. "She'll be really quiet. Mr Hardwood won't even see her."

Mrs Peasgood grinned. "All right," she said. Then Mrs Kaur came in to get the Bangla dancers together, and it was all go.

Assembly was special on Tuesdays. Sometimes it was a class assembly, sometimes it was one of Mr Hardwood's big presentations, which often featured his dad's old miner's helmet and boots (People Who Help Us), or his maracas and bullfight posters (Customs of Other Countries including Cruelty to Animals), or simply Mr Hardwood shouting for a long time with flecks of spittle showering the first three rows (People in This School Who Show No Consideration for Others). But today it was Multicultural, with four main items:

How Anansi Got Out of a Fix,
Rama and Sita (again),
Edith Cavell, The Heroic First World War Nurse
(Mr Hardwood's favourite)
and Mrs Kaur's Brilliant Bangla Dancers.

On a good day, a Multicultural Assembly would get you through at least half the morning. Billy usually looked forward to it, but he was slightly anxious today. He had recently been promoted to second drummer for the Bangla dancers, which meant a good deal of being looked at, and also he was going to have to leave Giulietta entirely to Mrs Peasgood's care. But everything went well.

Anansi Got Out of his Fix in great style, featuring the skills of Winston Clyde on the trampette. Rama and Sita rambled through their puzzling adventures towards their happy ending; no matter how may times Billy heard the story he had never been able to follow the plot. Edith Cavell refused the blindfold yet again, and was shot dead, not for the first time, by Mr Hardwood's trusty starter's pistol. And throughout all of this, Giulietta the Italian Greyhound lay quietly under Mrs Peasgood's chair, undisturbed by the bangs and screams, and unnoticed by anyone.

Then it was time for Mrs Kaur's Brilliant Bangla Dancers. Billy could see them out of the corner of his eye, shifting from one foot to the other in the wings, trying to keep their bangles quiet. Some of them had tablecloths tied round their waists and bright handkerchiefs round their heads. One or two of them, like Pritti, had the whole outfit, sent all the way from India. Scott Barnacle had his dad's old love beads round his ankle. His dad had been one of the Love Generation in the Seventies, he said, and though all that was over now, he was glad to see his love beads getting into the action again.

"Billy Webb," hissed Mrs Kaur. Billy jumped. His mind had been wandering. He glanced across at Wayne Ratkin, who was squatting over his drum glaring at Billy. Wayne Ratkin took his drumming very seriously. Mrs Kaur and Mrs Peasgood were proud of Ratkin's work on the drums and hoped it was his route to becoming a good and useful boy. Mr Hardwood was more sceptical and took the view that the Bangla drums just gave Ratkin more practice in hitting things.

Mrs Kaur nodded to Wayne Ratkin, Wayne Ratkin nodded to Billy, and they were off: WHACK bonga bonga bonga WHACK bonga bonga bonga WHACK bonga WHACK! and the Bangla dancers streamed on to the stage, skipping and wheeling and jangling their bangles, snapping their fingers over their heads and stamping their feet:

WHACK jingle bonga bonga WHACK! Scott Barnacle was like a boy possessed, inventing new jumps and turns as he went along, but never losing the rhythm, his Dad's love beads whirling round his ankles and his face red as a beetroot. WHACK skitter WHACK skitter JUMP THUMP WHACK bonga bonga bonga skitter skitter WHACK!

And then suddenly there was a new sound, a half-stifled squawk from the direction of Mrs Peasgood's chair, and something like a flash of grey lightning streaked through the front rows of the audience. It was Giulietta the Italian Greyhound! She skipped up on to the stage, reared up daintily on her hind legs, and weaved in and out amongst the dancers.

A great roar of laughter went up from the kids of Splott Street School. The Bangla Dancers were always good fun, but a Bangla Dancing Dog was something else again. Mrs Peasgood jumped up, very pink in the face, made a move towards the stage, and then sat down again. Billy's head felt hot and his ears buzzed, and he lost the rhythm for a moment, but Wayne Ratkin mever missed a beat: WHACK bonga bonga bonga WHACK bonga WHACK! and Billy's fingers responded: WHACK bonga bonga bonga WHACK bonga WHACK!

The laughter died down: now there was mostly silence, punctuated by little gasps of amazement, because Giulietta the Italian Greyhound wasn't ruining the Bangla dancing. She was the star of it. Pirouetting lightly on her slim hind legs, she threaded her way in and out of the whirling dancers, the little silver bell on her red leather collar adding a clear tinkling counterpoint to the rhythm; and her diamond studs glittered in the lights.

Billy sneaked a look at Mr Hardwood. His jaw had dropped open and his face was pale. Parents were invited along to Special Assemblies, and though only four had shown up today, word would get round very soon that things were getting slack at Splott Junior. And uninvited dogs invading the Multicultural Assembly was worse than things getting slack; it smacked very strongly of things getting out of control. Someone was going to have to do something about it. Mr Hardwood was going to have to do something about it.

He strode purposefully on to the stage and made a grab for Giulietta's collar. As soon as he'd done this he realised he had made a mistake. Giulietta slipped sideways, without losing a beat, and as Mr Hardwood stumbled forward, she turned and leapt right over his back. A great cheer went up. Mr Hardwood made a second grab. This time Giulietta rolled on her back, wriggled through his legs, and was safe on the far side of Pritti Shah before Mr Hardwood could turn round. Another great cheer. Then Mr Hardwood did something very sensible. He listened for the beat and raised his arms above his head. Forcing a tortured grin, he snapped his fingers and skipped once to the right, once to the left, and managed a clumsy do-si-do with Oninka Small. Then he gave a little bow and walked back to his chair, followed by ecstatic applause. Dogs and headmasters dancing on the same stage! This was one brilliant assembly!

Mrs Kaur's Bangla dancers had already gone on much

longer than their usual performance, but it wasn't over yet, far from it. Wayne Ratkin had the Red Mist. Eyes narrowed to tiny slits, he was whacking his drum as hard as he'd ever whacked anything: WHACK bonga bonga bonga WHACK bonga WHACK bonga WHACK WHACKA WHACK! Billy picked up the new fierce rhythm and the dancers whirled faster and faster, some of them spinning giddily right off the sides of the stage; but right in the centre were Scott Barnacle, his face more like a red traffic light than a beetroot now, and Giulietta the Italian Greyhound. Scott was whirling round on one leg with the other held out straight, and every time his leg whirled round, Giulietta jumped straight over it, sometimes forwards, sometimes backwards, sometimes turning right over in a somersault.

Billy was just wondering how long it would all go on, when Wayne Ratkin opened his eyes and stared desperately across at him. It was clear that if they didn't stop soon, Ratkin would self-destruct or disappear up his own drum. Billy gave the slowing down nod: WHACK Bonga WHACK bonga bonga. . . bonga . . . bonga . . . WHACK! On a sudden inspiration, Scott Barnacle gasped:

"Giulietta . . . hop-la!" and Giulietta leapt neatly on to his shoulders and balanced there on her hind legs, waving her front paws at the audience. The Bangla Dancing was over.

It seemed very quiet in Mr Hardwood's office. Mr Hardwood was sitting behind his desk, looking grim. Billy was standing where the bad kids always stand, on the middle of Mr Hardwood's posh rug. Mrs Peasgood was sitting on the hard brown visitor's chair. And Giulietta was lying curled demurely around Mrs Peasgood's feet.

"Not on, this," said Mr Hardwood eventually. "I've known things like this cause international incidents."

"Mrs Kaur didn't mind," said Mrs Peasgood. "I think it went down really well, honestly."

"Hmm," said Mr Hardwood. "Not the point. What's this boy's name?"

"Billy Webb," said Mrs Peasgood. "He's in my class."

"New, is he? New, are you, son?"

"No, Mr Hardwood," said Billy. "I've been here since the Infants."

"Never seen you before in my life," said Mr Hardwood with utter conviction. "Here to make trouble, are you, Billy Webb? Because if you are, you've got another thing coming!"

Billy decided not to reply to this.

"I think everyone appreciated the way you joined in

the dancing, Mr Hardwood," said Mrs Peasgood tactfully.

"You don't hold down a job like this for ten years without developing a knack for that sort of thing," said Mr Hardwood, slightly mollified. "But it wasn't my choosing, I can tell you that. This boy and his dog have held a Multicultural Assembly up to ridicule!"

"But she is multicultural," said Billy without meaning to.

"Half-wit, are you boy? Don't you know the meaning of a simple word like multicultural?"

"He means the dog's Italian," said Mrs Peasgood quickly. "She's an Italian greyhound, and I understand she does actually come from Italy, doesn't she, Billy?"

"She's on an international exchange," said Billy brilliantly. Mr Hardwood's jaw dropped open again and Mrs Peasgood flashed him a warning glance. Clearly he was getting too full of himself again. Or someone else.

"Trying to be clever with me, boy?" said Mr Hardwood.

"No, sir," said Billy, suppressing the thought (who had put it there?) that maybe being clever, or trying to be clever, was what school was all about, or ought to be.

"Because let me tell you, I don't draw Special Needs funding for dancing dogs, from Italy or Timbuktu!"

"We really didn't know she'd do anything like that,

did we, Billy? It was my fault for letting her go, I was sure she'd gone to sleep," said Mrs Peasgood. Billy said nothing but felt rather uneasy. He had just remembered Alfonso's remark that though Giulietta was not a fighter or a biter, she was a bit of a dancer.

"Well," said Mr Hardwood. "I'm going to confiscate this dog."

"You can't do that," said Billy anxiously. "I'm looking after her for a friend."

"Listen to me, son," said Mr Hardwood, letting one huge fist drop heavily on to his desk. "You may be new here, but you'll soon learn that they call this school Mr Hardwood's school. That means, what I say goes!"

Billy felt bad. What was he going to say to Alfonso Bonzo? What was going to happen to Giulietta? What was going to happen to Fred?

"But if," said Mr Hardwood, remembering his legal position, "if you keep your nose clean for the rest of the day and this dog behaves itself. . . "

"Herself," said Mrs Peasgood, "and I'm sure she will, Mr Hardwood."

"If she behaves herself . . . I might let you have her back at home time; and if I do, I don't want to see her in my school again."

Billy was very worried for the rest of the day, but took some comfort from seeing that Mrs Peasgood didn't seem worried at all, and he sensed that she cared for Giulietta just as much as he did. It was an odd sort of day. Mrs Peasgood and several other teachers took frequent absences from their classrooms, coming back smiling, and Nigel Creamer, whose weak bladder meant that he took frequent absences as well, reported that he'd seen three teachers listening outside Mr Hardwood's door. Creamer managed to listen himself for a moment or two. He said it sounded as if Mr Hardwood had gone all soft and found himself a girlfriend. He had someone in there anyway, and he was calling her baby and love and darling and all stuff like that.

In the afternoon Mr Hardwood neglected his form-filling for the Education Office, and instead undertook a lengthy Safety Inspection of the school grounds, accompanied by Giulietta. They tested the safety of the climbing frame for half an hour, and then they tested the safety of the Grassy Slope by rolling down it about twenty times.

At home time, Billy was summoned to Mr Hardwood's room again. He knocked and went in. Mr Hardwood was sitting behind his desk, with Giulietta in his lap. She was nibbling gently at one of his ears.

"Ah, give over, lass," said Mr Hardwood tenderly, but Giulietta didn't, and Mr Hardwood didn't seem to mind a bit.

"Nice little dog, that," said Mr Hardwood to Billy. "My dad had whippets, you know."

"She's not a whippet, Mr Hardwood."

"I know she's not a whippet. I was just saying my dad had whippets. Um. . . this friend of yours, he wouldn't be thinking of selling this dog, would he?"

"No," said Billy.

"Ah, well," said Mr Hardwood. "You can tell him from a man who knows about these things, he's got a very nice little dog there. Yes."

Mr Hardwood frowned thoughtfully for a bit and then seemed to come to a decision .

"Billy Webb," he said. "I'm going to show you something I don't show to everyone."

He slid open the top drawer of his desk and took out two rounded grey objects. Silently he held them up to Billy and turned them round and round in his hands.

"Know what these are?" said Mr Hardwood. "They're my dad's hip joints. Think on."

It was a quarter to six and Billy Webb was worried again. On the way home he had heard a low melodious whistle, just two notes. He had turned, expecting to see Alfonso Bonzo, but Splott Street was empty, apart from Scott Barnacle's small sister June carrying home some dandelions for Rod Stewart, her rabbit. When Billy turned round again, Giulietta had gone.

Now he was sitting at the kitchen table eating bacon sandwiches with his dad and his sister, worrying about Fred. He felt really dreadful. Giulietta had been a Really Good Swap, but Alfonso had got her back, and it looked as if he had Fred for Keepsies. The Italian Exchange Student had gone back on the deal. He had Fred, and Billy had nothing; and it was all Billy's fault. Only this morning he had told Alfonso Bonzo that you just didn't swap dogs. Dogs aren't like things, dogs are like people. Why hadn't he stuck to it? What was happening to poor old Fred? How could he explain it to the family? Fred wasn't just Billy's dog, even though Billy took him for most of his walks. He was the family dog. His mum slept with him when his dad was on night shift. Linda confided in him; spent hours in her room telling him things about boys. His dad liked to have Fred around, and took him to the pub every Friday night and Sunday morning. Billy began to realize that he'd done something terribly wrong.

He looked around the table. It all seemed so terribly normal. Mum, Dad, Linda, Billy, eating this great pile of bacon sandwiches. Billy had read in books about people who were desperately worried and sad, sitting at the table unable to eat a thing. It didn't seem to work that way with him. He had eaten seven bacon sandwiches already, cramming them down in a desperate absent-minded sort of way, because he couldn't think of anything else to do. Any minute now, someone was going to say, "Where's Fred?", or, "Haven't seen old Fred about," and they would look at Billy, and his face would go hot then pale, his ears would buzz, and the seven bacon sandwiches would rise up from his gorge like a tidal wave, and. . .

Then he heard four firm scratches at the kitchen door. His mother got up.

"Must be old Fred," she said. "Thought it was funny, him not showing up at teatime."

She opened the door and Fred came in. He was dressed in a short double breasted brown barathea jacket, below which his sturdy brown and white lower parts looked particularly rude. On his head was a soft brown velour trilby hat, secured by an elastic band. He smelt very strongly of expensive men's cologne. And he was walking on his hind legs.

Mrs Webb stood holding the door open in gaping silence, and Linda, Dad, and Billy also stared silently as Fred, taking no notice of any of them, walked unsteadily past the kitchen table and over to the door to the hall, where he stood on his hind legs fiddling at the handle with his paws. Without thinking of what he was doing, Billy got up and opened the door for him. Fred nodded to him, as if to a casual acquaintance, and tottered through.

"Did you see what I just saw?" said Billy's dad. They all got up and went to the door. Fred was in the hall, still on his hind legs, posing in front of the hall mirror.

"Fred!" squealed Linda. "What's come over you?" Fred turned and stared at her as if he'd never seen her before. Then he looked at Billy and his mother and father, and a curious embarrassed look came over not only his face but his whole body. He dropped on to his forepaws and scratched at the brown velour hat till it fell on the floor, where he stared at it in amazement. Then he scrabbled at the brown barathea jacket with his hind legs until the buttons popped and he could pull it off with his teeth. Then, with his tail between his legs, he slouched back into the kitchen, keeping his belly low to the floor, went in his bed, turned round three times, and lay with his face to the wall pretending to be asleep.

"Billy," said his mother, "D'you know anything about this?"

They all looked at Billy. His face went red, then pale. He waited for the next stage. But the bacon sandwiches just gave a lurch, then stayed where they were.

"Well," said Billy Webb, "you're not going to believe this."

The Milanese Television Set

"It's a good story," said Billy's father when he had finished, "but speaking for myself, I'll believe this Alfonso Bonzo when I see him."

"Probably you won't see him, though," said Billy.

"Yes, that's what I thought," said his dad, going over to the TV to turn the Test Match on.

"I wouldn't mind seeing him," said Billy's mum. "I'd have a few words to say to him. I'd ask him who he thinks he is, going round confusing other people's dogs. Look at Fred there. He's been really upset, that dog has. It isn't right."

"Oh, Mum," said Linda. "Billy was having you on."

"No, I wasn't," said Billy.

"Just trying to wind us all up, and he's still doing it."

"Well how did poor Fred get dressed up like that then?" said Mrs Webb. "You don't think he went down the shops and bought all those clothes, do you?"

"Well, how should I know? Probably one of Billy's mates did it."

"Was it one of your mates, Billy?" asked his mother.

"In a way," he said. "He is sort of a mate."

"Who?"

"Alfonso Bonzo"

"Look, how old is he, this Italian mate of yours?"

"I don't know," said Billy.

"Older than you, though?"

"Oh, yes. Much older. More than twenty, anyway."

"I don't like the sound of this at all," said Mrs Webb. "You know about men who come up to little boys and talk to them, you've been told often enough."

"He's not like that," said Billy with utter certainty.

"Well, I don't like the sound of this at all," said his mother. "Next time he comes, if he comes, you tell him I want a word with him. And your dad wants a word with him. And no more swaps. Time you were growing out of that. All right?"

"All right," said Billy.

The front doorbell rang and Linda went to answer it. It was usually for Linda, like the telephone was usually for Linda. She had a lot of girl friends and usually one or two boy friends on the go.

Billy could feel his mum giving him one of her searching looks. Sometimes he felt he knew too many women with searching looks. He kept his eyes down on the plate. He had had enough searching looks in the last couple of days to last him a lifetime.

"Mum! Billy! It's him!"

Billy's mother got up and went into the hall. Fred pricked up his ears, but continued to lie still with his face to the wall; Fred had clearly had enough excitement for one day. Billy's dad didn't take his eyes off the TV. The England Number Five batsman had just got in and he didn't want to miss any sixes. And Billy just kept staring at his plate.

Mother and daughter came back into the room, both looking a bit pink and flustered. Alfonso Bonzo was with them.

"Good evening!" said Alfonso Bonzo, smiling round the room. "How do you do, Alfonso Bonzo my name, just a little social call."

"Evening," said Billy's dad, not getting up. "Er, Test Match." He turned round again.

"You mustn't mind Mr Webb," said Billy's mum. She still looked flustered. "He's not a great one for socialising."

Billy kept his eyes down, his brain whirling. What was

going on? Why were they so strange? His dad hadn't even believed in Alfonso Bonzo, he ought to be staring at him in amazement instead of staring at the telly. And his mum was supposed to be giving Alfonso Bonzo a piece of her mind, not flapping round with a pink face as if he were the vicar or Prince Charles or something. They couldn't be shy of Alfonso Bonzo, surely? He risked a quick look at Linda. She didn't seem so shy now. She was having a really good look at Alfonso Bonzo. She looked very interested but also amused at the same time, as if she were thinking, "Who on earth is this crazy twit?" Then Alfonso turned one of his special smiles on her, and she blushed scarlet.

"I am sorry," he said. "I see I interrupt your meal. I am desolated. Please continue, don't mind Alfonso Bonzo."

"It's all right, really!" said Mrs Webb. "We'd all finished eating."

"No, no, please! I see you still have three beautiful bacon sandwiches left. Brilliant aroma! I see you are one ace cook, Mrs Webb!"

"Would you like one?" she said. "Fraid they'll be a bit cold now."

"For me? Really? You mean it? Alfonso Bonzo loves a bacon butty!"

They watched him eat. He ate with the enthusiasm of a very hungry man, and the elegance of a prince. When he had finished he sighed, closed his eyes, and kissed his fingers.

"Magnifico!" he said. "My mamma in Milano would be proud to make such a bacon sandwich. Billy Webb, you are one very lucky boy, I think."

Billy looked at his mother. She had this sort of daft delighted look on her face. There would be no telling-off now, he knew. No piece of her mind. She had fallen under the spell of Alfonso's charm, or whatever it was he had, even faster than Billy had.

Alfonso started to talk, about his mamma and his sisters in Italia, about the joys and sorrows of being an Italian Exchange Student, about Freddo and what a fine and clever dog he was, and about Billy and what a fine and clever son he was. And every few moments he would glance across at Linda, and she'd smile and blush, and once or twice he looked over at Billy's dad, but Billy's dad never turned.

He had a good excuse. The English batsmen were in tremendous form, knocking the ball all over the place. Billy's dad was bouncing up and down in his chair as Australia's fastest bowler ran up to bowl.

Then the telly went dead. The sound died slowly, and the picture dwindled to a tiny dot, then nothing.

"Well, will you look at that!" said Billy's dad. He twiddled the knob. Nothing.

Alfonso was on his feet in an instant.

"Hey, Mr Webb, maybe I mend you that telly. Alfonso Bonzo one brilliant boy with TV sets, ace mechanic, no messing about!"

"Be great if you could, son," said Mr Webb.

Alfonso Bonzo fiddled around briefly at the back of the set. When he stood up his face was sad.

"I'm so sorry, Mr Webb, sir. This is a very sick TV you got here. You got big tube trouble. For that I have to take away, bring back. So sorry." Then his face lit up again. "Hey. I got it. I do you small exchange. You have Alfonso Bonzo's TV set one night, I take yours, bring it back tomorrow good as new. How you like that?"

"Well. Sounds all right to me. Thanks very much, Mr Bonzo," said Billy's dad.

"Alfonso, please."

"But it's such a lot of trouble for you, Alfonso," said Billy's mother.

"No trouble. Pleasure, for you."

"But what about you, won't you want yours?"

"I think maybe I don't watch TV tonight. Maybe go dancing. Now I fetch. Five minutes only. I go, I come back."

He went, and he came back, and it took less than five minutes. When the doorbell went again, there was a little Fiat van standing outside in the road, and Alfonso

Bonzo was tottering up the drive carrying the biggest TV set the Webb family had ever seen. In fact all you could see of Alfonso was his trousers; it looked as if an enormous telly with one yellow leg and one green leg was taking over the Webb household.

Alfonso tottered into the living room and set it down. It was nearly as tall as he was. It wasn't one of the flashy modern sets: in fact it reminded Billy of the Victorian wardrobe in his grandma's bedroom. It was made of gleaming polished walnut with beautifully matched graining, with other kinds of wood set into it in intricate patterns, and a mother-of-pearl design winding round the large screen. It had stout bandy legs like a bulldog's legs, with fat wooden paws and claws that looked like real ivory. Along the top was a beautiful curly scroll carved out of mahogany, with the legend LUIGI BELLONA, MILANO in gold leaf. The Webb family stared at it in stunned silence.

"Bit old-fashioned, this TV, but I think you find he work OK," said Alfonso. He switched it on. Nobody except Billy seemed to notice that Alfonso didn't plug it in or connect an aerial. The mad hippy didn't think it would work without mains electricity, did he?

But it did. The picture took a long while to form, as it often does with old sets, but when it settled it was beautiful. It looked more like a painting by an old master than a TV picture. The grass on the outfield looked like real growing grass, with all sorts of subtle shadings from sharp yellowy-green to deep foggy purple; and in the close-up that followed you could see the scuffed grain on the seam of the bruised-red cricket ball as the mighty Australian paceman rubbed it up and down on his powerful thigh.

Billy's dad did not go in for fancy descriptions and elaborate praise. "Nice picture, Alfonso, thanks a lot," he said, and sat down to watch it. Billy and Linda went back to the kitchen to stack the dishes and wash up. Alfonso didn't follow them. He drew Mrs Webb aside for a whispered conversation in the passage. Billy didn't altogether like this, he wasn't sure why. Alfonso was getting into too many things, and somehow that wasn't comfortable. Still. Nothing Billy Webb could do about it. He ran the hot tap and squirted washing up liquid in the bowl. He always washed and Linda always dried.

Alfonso came into the kitchen and picked up a tea-towel. "Hey, Linda," he said. "How you like to come dancing with Alfonso Bonzo tonight? I ask your mamma and she say OK, if I get you home by midnight, and you want to go with me."

Linda blushed and bit her lip. She dried two plates before she answered.

"No thanks," she said. "Washing my hair tonight."

"But your hair is beautiful!" said Alfonso Bonzo. "What's the matter, you don't like dancing?"

"Course I like dancing," she said.

"You don't like Alfonso Bonzo?"

"You're all right," she said grudgingly.

"Then whatsa the problem?"

Linda dried three more plates, biting her lip so hard that she left dents in it. Billy kept his head down over the foam, wishing he were somewhere else. It was really embarrassing. And one day, he supposed, he would be in for all this stuff, plucking up the courage to ask girls out, finding somewhere to go, thinking of something to do, all the blushing and lip biting and misunderstandings and tears and slammed front doors. What was it that could be worth all that? Nothing. He liked looking at Pritti Shah, and even talking to her in a way, but he was always glad when the talking stopped and he could get on with his life again. And as for getting dressed up and going out with her!!! No, he'd be the exception, when he got older. He'd just look, and then get on with his life. Swaps, deals, sensible things like that.

"It's your gear," said Linda eventually. "I'm sorry, don't mean to be rude, but you did ask."

"My gear? I don't understand. My little van not very smart, but she got four forward gear, one reverse gear, all work very well, no problem."

"No, I meant your clothes, what you're wearing. I couldn't go out with anyone dressed like that. Sorry."

Alfonso Bonzo smiled a beautiful smile of understanding and forgiveness.

"Ah, capisco! You don't want to make a spectacle of yourself, dancing with a mad hippy man! No problem! This what you call, this gear, this just Alfonso's working gear; when I come and call for you you see me in nice dancing clothes, ace brilliant disco suit, you be proud, I promise!"

"Well," she said. "Don't want anything weird."

"Nothing weird," he promised. "Alfonso Bonzo blend into the background."

Linda smiled. "Don't see that happening," she said.

"Eight o'clock," said Alfonso Bonzo "I go, I come back, and we have one brilliant time!"

When he'd finished the washing up, Billy went into the living room for another look at the Italian TV. His father had gone up the road to the betting shop to collect his winnings on a horse he'd been tipped off about at work. His mother had taken Fred for a run in the park in the hope that the fresh air would dissipate some of his embarrassing smell; and Linda was upstairs in the bathroom starting to prepare for her evening out.

The Milanese Television squatted alone in the bay window, with all the presence and power of an elderly aunt or a large sleeping animal. It was still not plugged in; and when Billy peered round the back of it he couldn't see any cables to plug it in with. It couldn't possibly work. Yet it had worked. He had seen it working. Or had he? It might have been some sort of dream.

Feeling rather foolish, he pressed the "ON" switch, and then the BBC2 button. There was a faint hum, and then the picture swirled into life. Just as vivid as before: shimmering rippling grass, blue shadows lengthening, a big round drop of sweat trembling on the bowler's forehead as he turned to start his run-up. Billy wasn't actually all that interested in cricket, but it looked so bright and real on Alfonso Bonzo's TV that he was held fascinated by it.

Then he saw the extra button. There were the usual four that you get on old-fashioned TV sets. And this extra one. 3D. Billy pressed it.

Suddenly he seemed to be running down the pitch just behind the bowler. The sounds of the crowd were all around him, and close to him he could hear heavy harsh breathing and the pounding of size eleven cricket boots on the hard turf. The England Number Five batsman stood twenty metres or so away, but looking much closer, balanced like a big cat, a grin starting to form on his sweating face as he lifted his bat. There was a huge rasping grunt that seemed to come from right inside Billy as the bowler let the ball go, and then he was halfway down the pitch, much too dangerously close to batsmen as the heavy bat swept down and followed through with tremendous force.

Billy couldn't help turning his head away for a split second. When he looked again, he wasn't in the middle of the field, he was in the crowd, with loud shouts and the clanking of beer cans all round him. People were putting their arms across their heads and ducking away from him. It was weird: he was in his own living room, and at the same time standing on a green wooden bench in the evening sunshine at the Oval cricket ground. Then he saw why the people were ducking and dodging. High in the air, and plummetting down towards him, was a red leather sphere, dark against the sky but so clear and three-dimensional that Billy could see the seam spinning and catching the light. Someone shouted "Look out, son!" but he couldn't move. Without any conscious thought, he cupped both hands together in front of him and screwed his face up. Suddenly the ball got bigger and bigger, and he wanted to run, but it was too late. Then something fierce and heavy smacked into his hands, and his fingers closed instinctively round it. He had caught the ball.

The cheering all round him was deafening now,

buzzing in his ears and making him dizzy, but he. still couldn't move. People were laughing and patting him on the back. Then one of the Australian fielders trotted over to the boundary fence. His face was very brown and his teeth looked unnaturally white under his green cap as he grinned up at Billy.

"Can we have our ball back, please, son?" he said, and everybody laughed again. Billy wordlessly tossed the ball to him, and there was another laugh. Billy's hands were burning and throbbing now. It was all too much. He wanted it to stop. He felt giddy and the sun was dazzling his eyes.

Then the picture changed to a shot of the sightscreen, with the batsman's score going up from 224 to 230. Billy found that he could move again. He crept across to the Milanese TV set and pressed one of the buttons, and he was no longer at the Oval, but back in his own living room. He sank thankfully into his dad's easy chair.

As soon as he'd done it, he realized that what he should have done was press the 3D button off, or turn the set off altogether; but BBC1 on 3D was much easier to cope with. For a start, although what was on the screen was far more vivid that any ordinary TV picture, it wasn't leaping about and looming like the Test Match, and it wasn't hurtling towards him at a hundred miles an hour. Billy was sitting on one side of the living room in his dad's familiar chair, and on the other side of the room was a big desk with a man sitting behind it, a man Billy knew from somewhere, talking in a pleasant but boring way about a pay claim the teachers were making, and whether they'd go on strike or not. Billy didn't think there was much chance of a strike at Splott Street Junior. It was very hard to imagine Mr Hardwood and Mrs Peasgood doing anything drastic like going on strike, unfortunately. It was hard to imagine them doing anything except what they did in school. He knew they must have a private life, Mrs Peasgood especially, but he couldn't picture them actually at it, even simple things like brushing their teeth and going to bed. What sort of pyjamas would old Hardwood wear? Perhaps they would have pictures of whippets or miner's lamps. When he'd been in the Infants Billy had thought that the teachers all lived in the school and went to bed with their clothes on, under their tables.

This newsreader on the telly was the same sort of person. He was still just sitting there reading the news in his pleasant boring voice. The only difference was that he thought he was in a TV studio hundreds of kilometres away, and instead he was sitting at his desk boring on about his strikes and things in Billy's living room. Scott Barnacle's dad had once told Billy and Scott that because it was so hot in the studios, the newsreaders only wore the top half of their suits – if you could see behind the desks you'd see they were all in their underpants. Daft. Couldn't be true, could it? But it was nice to think about . . . wonder if there was anything in it?

Billy suddenly realized that he had the means to prove it one way or the other, with Alfonso Bonzo's 3D Milanese TV set. He got very quietly out of his chair. The newsreader took no notice, although he was looking right at Billy every time he lifted his eyes from his script. Billy tiptoed up to his desk, and then round to the side of it, expecting to be dragged away by the scruff of his neck every second. But nothing happened and the newsreader droned on; he had changed the subject to world food and population concerns now. Now Billy was behind the desk with him. He could see the script, with all the important words underlined in yellow highlighter. Then he looked down, and gasped. It was true! Beneath his formal dark grey jacket and smart shirt and tie, the newsreader was wearing striped boxer shorts with his initials on, and he had suspenders to hold his socks up. And he had very hairy legs indeed. Billy crept back to his chair. Wait till Scott Barnacle heard about this. Wait till Scott Barnacle's dad heard about this! The BBC News would never seem the same again.

The newsreader, though he seemed to be smiling

pleasantly at Billy all the time, didn't seem to be bothered in the least about being in a front room in Splott Street with boys taking crafty peeps at his stripy pants.

"Concern is growing in the Sudan," he said to Billy, "that the desperately needed relief supplies are not going to get through soon enough to save the starving people." He paused and frowned slightly. "Our film report contains material which some viewers may find distressing." He looked down at his papers, and then suddenly he'd gone, desk and all, sucked back into the insides of the Milanese TV set. The whole programme had gone back into the set, to Billy's great relief, though it was still painfully vivid and real. People, thin black people, as far as the eye could see, on a flat plain. There was nothing else. No houses, no shelter, no food. The people were very quiet. A few of them were moving about very slowly, but most of them were lying down or squatting motionless. You could see there was a breeze blowing, because it caught at the corners of the blankets and the torn sand-coloured jumpers they were wearing, exposing their arms and legs, thin as bent twigs. Some of them had babies. They were quiet and still too. Billy suddenly thought that some of them might be dead. The mothers might be too tired and weak to notice. Or perhaps they did know, and they were holding on to the babies because they didn't know what else to do with them. It was awful, the silence. Someone should be talking about how help was on its way, how things were going to be all right for these people.

A fly was buzzing round the living room. It came to rest on Billy's ear, and he brushed it away. To his horror, he saw it fly towards the TV set and land on the screen. No, it hadn't landed on the screen, the screen wasn't solid any more, it was like an open window on to the desert, and the fly buzzed through it and landed on a woman's face. She didn't brush it off. She just let it crawl about on her face, till it stood still on her eyelid, rubbing its front legs together. The fly he had brushed off his ear. His fly. Now it was a tiny extra part of her troubles.

Now he was looking at a boy. It was impossible to tell how old the boy was. He was sitting on the ground looking up at Billy. He was very close. Billy knew that if he reached his hand forward through the screen he would be able to touch him. His head looked too heavy for his thin neck, and you could see all his bones through his skin. His face looked very tired, and very patient.

And then at last the voice started, but it didn't explain how help was on its way, and how things were going to be all right for this boy and the other people.

"This is Joseph," said the voice. It didn't come from the TV set: the man speaking sounded as if he was sitting on the arm of Billy's chair, talking quietly into his ear.

"Joseph is ten years old, but he weighs only as much as the average healthy four-year-old. He walked thirty kilometres to come here, because he was told there would be food and shelter here. There isn't any food and there isn't any shelter. Joseph is starving."

Joseph started trying to get up. It looked impossible that his thin legs, thin as the legs of an insect, could carry him. But he pushed steadily and patiently, looking at Billy all the time. Then he started to take a couple of wavering steps towards Billy. In a moment he would be out of the screen, dying on the living room carpet. Billy heard a moaning sound, and he knew that he had made it himself. With one hand over his eyes, he groped forward for the OFF button and pressed it. He opened his eyes again. Joseph had dwindled to a tiny dot. The dot disappeared. Joseph had gone.

Billy stood very still. The world seemed to be going away from him. The walls of the living room bulged outwards and wobbled, and he felt sweat suddenly forming in cold lumps all over his forehead. His shirt felt wet and cold against his body and he shivered. His legs were weak. He reached for the back of his dad's easy chair and gripped on to it hard. After a moment the walls stopped wobbling and straightened themselves up again. The Milanese television set squatted silently in the bay window. The world, the frightening world, had gone back into it.

It was very quiet in the house, but outside he could hear the reassuring sound of Splott Street. Darnell Masuda's dad trying to start his old Cortina, Scott Barnacle's mum yelling to Scott to go down the corner shop for her. It he went out, he would be part of it; he could give Mr Masuda a push, or he could walk down to the corner shop with Scott Barnacle. There were no dead babies in Splott Street, no boys of his own age so weak with hunger that they couldn't stand up.

It was good knowing that he could go out there and be ordinary if he wanted to. And he did want to; but something else was more important. He had to have a proper think about some of the things that had been happening. And he didn't want to do that in the same room as that big fat Milanese television set. He went out into the hall and walked slowly upstairs, past the whirring hair dryer behind Linda's closed door, and into his own safe familiar room, with all its old pictures and posters and books and useful swaps lined up on the shelf.

There were two good places for thinking: in the bath,

or lying on his bed. A couple of years ago he had been in the bath when it had suddenly come to him that he didn't believe in God or any of that stuff; and that had been such a frightening thought that he'd actually yelled for his dad. And his dad had told him that he didn't believe in God either. No one knew for certain, but his dad said his opinion was that people just imagined God to cheer themselves up. He couldn't see any use in God himself, it was up to people to help each other, not expect some old bloke in white robes to sort them out.

It had been a real comfort at the time, when his dad had said that. Knowing that it wasn't weird or wicked not to believe in God, that other people felt the same. And after that he had noticed that some of the teachers, Mrs Peasgood for one, didn't close their eyes and say the Lord's Prayer out loud when Mr Hardwood did. But that still left problems. People helping each other worked all right in his family, and some of the time in school, even. But who was going to help Joseph? He hadn't helped Joseph. He had switched him off and sent him back to die in the Milanese television set because he couldn't bear the thought of him dying on the living room carpet.

It wasn't fair. It was terrible. And he couldn't really see how it was his fault. When the appeals had come round school, he had given things, just like most other people;

more than most, in fact, because he had the proceeds of his swaps and deals as well as his pocket money. But it hadn't got through in time. If there was a God, well, he had a lot to answer for, hadn't he?

And Alfonso Bonzo, didn't he have a lot to answer for as well? He was so nice and friendly and easy to get on with, and he kept his promises, or he had done so far, but there was always something extra, always something strange, always something, well . . . dangerous about Alfonso Bonzo's exchanges. Billy hoped Linda was going to be all right, going out with Alfonso Bonzo. He would have liked to warn her or something, but there wasn't anything definite to warn her against; and anyway he knew she wouldn't take any notice. She often took her time making her mind up about something, but once she had made up her mind, that was it. She was the one who'd decided to leave school and go to work in Timball's woodyard, despite what the teachers and Mum and Dad had said; and if she changed her mind and went to college that would be her decision too. She wouldn't be impressed with anything Billy said about Alfonso Bonzo

But Alfonso was different. He wasn't just the best swapper of all time. He had some sort of special powers, a bit like magicians and gods were supposed to have, and he seemed to use them just for fun, or for mischief, just to amuse himself. And for some reason he had picked on Billy and his family. For some reason? No use trying to wriggle out of it. Billy knew the reason. The swapping. He was a bit of an exchange student himself. He had a bit of Alfonso Bonzo in him.

How long ago had the whirring of the hair dryer stopped? Billy looked at his watch. It was nearly eight o'clock. He had been lying on the bed thinking for nearly an hour and a half, and he hadn't come to any important decisions. He was just going to have to play things by ear. One thing he knew, though: no more swaps with Alfonso. Whatever it was that came next after the Milanese television set, he wanted nothing to do with it. He had gone as far as he wanted to, further than he wanted to, with Alfonso Bonzo; and fascinating as the Italian Exchange Student was, Billy wanted him out of his life now.

Then the doorbell rang. Billy heard Linda's bedroom door open, and her quick footsteps going down the stairs. He looked out of the window. The little Fiat van was outside, and Alfonso Bonzo was standing on the pavement. He was wearing a beautiful cream-coloured linen suit, and a dark green shirt with an intricate design of climbing monkeys on it. His cream leather casual shoes matched his suit, and their gold buckles caught the light. Billy could see that Alfonso's posh clothes met with his sister's approval: she was smiling into Alfonso's face as he opened the door of the van for her and settled her into his seat. Alfonso Bonzo walked round the van and opened the driver's door. Just before getting in, he looked up at Billy's window. The smile he flashed up at Billy was like strawberries and cream, and he winked at Billy as if there was something delightful and mysterious that only the two of them knew about. Then he got in the van and drove Linda away into the night.

The River of No Return

"He'll be all right, won't you, Billy?" said his dad.

"Yeah, course, I'll be all right," said Billy. Actually he rather wished his parents weren't going out, but he couldn't think of any good reason for saying so.

"He's a bit young to be left home alone," said his mother.

"Well, he knows where we are, it's only two minutes away, and he can give us a ring if anything crops up. And he's got Fred, they'll look after each other, like."

"It's OK," said Billy. "Don't fuss." And there really wasn't any need to fuss. They were just going out for a drink, the Intrepid Fox was only on the corner. They'd done it before, and they knew Billy was a sensible boy who was quite fond of his own company.

"Anyway, we won't be late," said his mother. "Want to be back in plenty of time for the Late Night Movie."

"*River of No Return*," said his father.

"Robert Mitchum," explained his mother, closing her eyes and sighing in an exaggerated way.

"Marilyn Monroe," countered his Dad. "Worrr!"

"So you be in bed by ten, and fast asleep by the time we get back, right?" said his mother.

"Yeah, all right," said Billy.

Then they went.

Billy didn't feel like watching the Milanese television, even without the 3D knob. He didn't feel like reading either. Looking along his shelf of books and comics, he couldn't see one that would have the power to take him over so that he could lose himself in it and forget about everything. He wasn't much of a boy for hobbies either. Since the days of Webb's Mouse Farm he'd never kept a stamp collection or a chemistry set or a soldering kit or a bow and arrows long enough to develop an addiction for it. There had always been someone who was in the market for a swap. He didn't really feel like just lying about thinking, either. He had had enough of that for one evening. He felt vaguely nervous and apprehensive, but he couldn't think of a good reason why. What he really dreaded was Alfonso Bonzo coming back while his parents were out, but he wouldn't do that, would he?

He was busy dancing the night away with Linda in his posh new suit, wasn't he?

In the end, Billy decided the best way to spend the evening was to do some very easy things. He roused Fred out of his bed in the kitchen and got him to come upstairs to his bedroom, and encouraged him to lie on the bed, which he wasn't usually allowed to do. Fred accepted the invitation gratefully: he looked as if he needed a good deal of uninterrupted sleep to get over his confusing day. Billy got into his pyjamas at half past eight, which was really babyishly early for him, but felt nice and comforting. He got out his *Harry Potter* tapes, which he hadn't played for ages, and set them going on the old cassette player in his bedroom. Then he got into bed with his Squirrel Nutkin jigsaw. It was a very old jigsaw, with real wooden pieces, from which the picture was peeling and fraying off in places. It had been his mother's jigsaw before it was Billy's, and somehow he had never really felt like swapping it. The pieces were very strangely shaped, not at all like ordinary jigsaw pieces, and a lot of people found it very hard to do. But Billy knew he could do it; he had done the Squirrel Nutkin every time he had been ill for years and years and years. Putting the bits in just where he knew they had to go made him feel strong and solid and competent. Alfonso Bonzo wasn't going to come. Alfonso Bonzo didn't exist really. If the whistling came down the road he wouldn't hear it. If the light knock came on the front door he wouldn't answer. He would just sit tight in his bed, with Fred snoring and dreaming, *Harry Potter* on the cassette player, and Squirrel Nutkin slowly taking shape on his lap.

He managed to think about nothing except Harry Potter and Squirrel Nutkin until he had put the last piece in, right in the middle of Nutkin's huge bushy tail. Then he heard the van again. He looked at his watch. Only half past ten. Alfonso Bonzo was supposed to be at the disco with Linda, they weren't supposed to be back till midnight; what if he had just gone off and left her there and come back to see Billy? Well, he couldn't get in if Billy didn't let him in, and Billy wasn't going to let him in. He had a good feeling that Fred didn't want to see him any more either. Fred was pretending to be still asleep, but Billy felt his body tensing, and the beginnings of a growl deep in his throat.

Then the front door opened and slammed shut, and Billy heard footsteps running up the stairs. Just one lot of footsteps. Linda's. He was sure of it. Then her bedroom door slammed, and he heard the van drive off.

"Linda?" he called.

No answer.

"Linda!"

Nothing.

He got out of bed and walked along the landing to the back bedroom, with Fred padding along behind him. He knocked softly on the door.

"What d'you want?"

He went in. Linda was sitting at the dressing table staring at herself in the mirror. She looked all right as far as Billy could see, but her face had a peculiar expression on it, much less sure of itself than it usually looked.

"You all right?" he said.

"Yeah," she said. "Course. Why shouldn't I be?"

"I dunno," he said. "You're early."

"What about it?"

"Wasn't it any good then?"

"I'm not going out with him again," she said.

"Why not?"

"Mind your own business."

"Wasn't he any good at dancing after all then?"

"Oh, yeah," she said. "He was good at dancing all right."

"What was it then?"

"Nothing," she said.

"Aw, come on, Linda."

"You wouldn't understand," she said. "But I'm not going out with him again, all right? Now go back to bed and take that dog with you, right?"

He stared at her for a bit, but he knew it was no good.

She never told him anything. Still, she seemed to be OK.

Nothing terrible seemed to have happened. And Alfonso Bonzo had gone away, maybe for good.

He went back to his bedroom and climbed into bed, and Fred climbed up next to him, but on top of the blankets instead of inside. Billy found to his surprise that he was really very tired. He put his arm round Fred's hard bulky body, and went straight to sleep.

It was one of those long rambling dreams, the sort you don't just wake up from feeling tired, but you actually find tiring while you're in them. In the dream he was having to trail-drive a great herd of mice along the Denver Trail to Milan. He ought to have been on a horse, he knew that, but the only mount he'd been able to borrow was Scott Barnacle's old BMX bike, which would not be fast enough to head the mice off if there was a stampede. All of the mice were at least as big as dogs, and some of them were as big as small cows, and they were very hard to drive: they wanted to go their own ways, and they turned and snarled if you pushed them along too hard. Fred was helping him, trotting along huffing and puffing and snapping at the big mice's heels, but the two of them weren't enough for a full-scale mouse drive, and he was too young to be in charge. They had to go through the Badlands, and Death Valley which was full of skeletons, where the scorching sun beat down all day and the nights were as cold as the North Pole. And now it was getting dark, and he could hear the howling of the coyotes unseen in the brush, and the low melodious whistles as the bad men signalled to each other, waiting for Billy to relax his concentration and fall asleep. He had to keep awake in this dream, he had to keep pedalling, keep the herd of mice moving along in a solid stream like a great grey river through the fearful night, and it was all too much, it wasn't fair, he was too young to be in charge of so much with only Fred to help him.

They must have got to Denver somehow, because he could hear laughing and doors slamming and people banging kettles on gas stoves, and he tried to call to the people to keep quiet, the mice were restless tonight, and sudden noises could stampede them, but his mother called up to him to go back to sleep, it was all right, they were home now, and he just managed to wake up enough to realize that he wasn't in Denver after all, he was in Splott Street, and he didn't have to drive the mice to Milan after all. With a great sigh, he rolled over and went back to sleep again, and this time he didn't dream.

Some time later, he awoke again. The dream was still there. He wasn't on the mouse drive any more, he was sitting up in bed rubbing his eyes. But Denver, or something like Denver, had come to Splott Street. It sounded like a Western saloon downstairs. There was music, a tinkling bar room piano with a lot of the notes out of tune, and hoarse shouting and laughter and the clink of glasses and the sound of heavy footsteps. Fred was sitting up as well, with his ears laid back on his head.

"What is it, Fred?" said Billy.

Fred growled low in the back of his throat.

Then Billy heard his mother laughing in the middle of all the noise. She sounded all right; she sounded as if she was having a good time. They must have brought some people back from the Intrepid Fox for a bit of a party. Not like his mum and dad, especially not in the middle of the week; they had to get up early just the same as he had to. He decided to go down and see what was going on. Maybe when they saw him they'd realize they were keeping him awake and turn down the record or whatever it was that was making the noise, and tell their friends it was time to go home. Anyway it would be interesting to see what they were all up to.

He got up and tiptoed down the stairs, with Fred padding softly behind him. There was more music now. A violin and an accordion had joined the out-of-tune piano, and they were playing a slow waltz tune, and the people weren't shouting and laughing so loudly. Maybe it would be mean to complain. It was the living room the noise was coming from, not the kitchen. That was odd. Usually when people came round after the pub they'd all be drinking coffee round the kitchen table.

Billy found he didn't want to go straight into the living room. He sat on the bottom step where he could see a thin strip of the room through a crack in the door. At first he couldn't make out what he was looking at. The carpet was the same, and he could see the green sofa, but the whole room seemed to have got bigger, with a high mahogany bar running the length of it, and a man standing behind the bar in a white shirt and with a big droopy old-fashioned moustache and a bald head. People were dancing in the room. Some of the women were wearing long dresses, and some of the men had big hats and cigars and guns at their belts. To think of them having a fancy-dress party without telling Billy about it! Not that Billy went in for fancy dress much, but he would have liked to be asked.

Then Billy saw his mother. She was dancing very slowly with a huge tall man, one of the biggest men Billy had ever seen. He had enormous wide shoulders like a boxing champion, and a great big face like a slab of rock, with high cheekbones and funny half-closed sleepy eyes, and his big chin had a huge dent in the front of it. The man was smiling in an absent-minded sort of way, but Billy could see how he was watching everything in the room through those half-closed sleepy eyes of his, as if he were ready for a fight at a second's notice. He looked a terribly dangerous man to deal with. But Billy's mother didn't seem to think so. She was dancing with her eyes shut and her face laid against the big stranger's chest, and she was smiling like someone smiling in her sleep. She looked young, too, and very pretty; something Billy had never thought before about his mother.

Billy shifted his position on the step: now he could see the whole of the sofa. And there was his father. He had a drink in his hand, and he was talking, waving his free hand about as he talked. Billy thought he had never seen his father talking so energetically before. Then he saw who his father was talking to. It was a woman in a red old-fashioned dress that showed a lot of her chest. She had startlingly bright blonde hair, and very wide blue eyes, like a sort of grown-up baby. She was smiling and laughing at everything his dad said, and looking into his eyes as if there were nowhere she would rather be in the world than where she was, and as if there were no one she would rather be with than his Dad. There was something familiar about her, too; Billy was sure he had seen her somewhere before, though he was pretty sure it hadn't been in Splott Street or anywhere round there. Then he remembered where he'd seen her. On the old calendar his Dad had tacked up in the garden shed. He even knew what her name was. Marilyn Monroe.

Billy felt very cold all of a sudden, and reached out for Fred. He knew what was happening now, and he knew he couldn't do anything about it, and he couldn't go into that strange new world in the living room. What he was watching was the Late Night Movie on TV, *River of No Return*, and it had spilled out of the Milanese television set and into his living room, because he had forgotten to switch off the knob that said 3D.

"Break a Leg"

Billy was awake. It didn't happen gradually, with that slow pleasant fumbling up towards the surface of life, but suddenly, with a jolt like a punch in the ribs that left him half sitting up in bed, panting, with a sick empty feeling in his solar plexus.

Well, he was alive, anyway, and he was in his own pyjamas in his own bed in his own bedroom. That was something. He felt exhausted and sick, though, with vague memories of having been on the Denver to Milan trail all night, and that he'd tried to get to the main saloon in town in time to stop the big shoot-out starting, but he'd been too late; still on the outskirts of the cardboard town with its garish lights, stranded on the dirt road with Fred and the vast herd of cowed and nervous mice milling round him, cut off from the terrible bar where people were swapping bullets, and exchanging life for death.

Oh, come on, Billy Webb. Only a dream. Awake now. Everything normal. Breakfast soon. Fred on the floor by the bed. Swaps set out in a line on the shelf. Linda's snoring taxi throbbing away in the back bedroom . . . wait a minute. Where were the little whimpers and the grunts and quacks from the front bedroom? He listened carefully. Nothing. Silence. He looked at his watch. Twenty to seven. His mum and dad were never up by this time, not when his dad was on day shift, which he was this week. Something must have happened to them. Something terrible. And in a flash, he knew what it was.

The tall stranger with the sleepy eyes and the cleft in his big chin must have challenged his dad to a shoot-out and gone off with his mother. Anyone could have seen that there was trouble brewing there, really serious trouble. And Billy had seen for himself how the Milanese television set could bring the terrors of the world spilling out of the frame of its screen, flooding the living room with things too hard to cope with. A hundred-kilometre-an-hour cricket ball. A starving African boy. Marilyn Monroe and Robert Mitchum: guns, jealousy, cruelty and fear.

Alfonso Bonzo with his brilliant smile and his magical exchanges had done all that. He had taken away Billy's mum and dad, and in a few minutes the whistling would start at the far end of the street, and Alfonso Bonzo would come back, and this time he'd be coming for Billy. What could he do? Get out of the house, that would be a start. Wake up Linda, take Fred, and go. But where?

Billy found he was thinking about Mrs Peasgood. He had a feeling that she had noticed some of the things that were happening, she had seen the amazing bag and she had met Giulietta, so she knew something about Alfonso Bonzo's power. But he didn't know where she lived. She didn't live in Splott Street or any of the streets round about. None of the teachers did except Mrs Kaur.

It was getting near seven. He had to do something. He got out of bed and went over to the window and made himself draw the curtains back, dreading that he would see Alfonso Bonzo standing quiefly on the pavement outside. But no. He wasn't there. The Milanese TV set was, its fat bulk squatting half on the pavement and half in the gutter, its screen blankly reflecting bricks and windows, its gleaming walnut flanks beaded with the morning dew. How had it got there?

And just at that moment, Billy heard the clink of cups and plates from downstairs, and smelt the smell of coffee. His mother's coffee. No one else made coffee that smelt the same as Billy's mother's coffee, no one else made it so strong and stewed it so long. It was truly gut-rotting coffee, Billy's mother's coffee, but Billy Webb was happier to smell it than he had ever been to smell anything. He pulled on his dressing gown and went down to the kitchen.

His father was sitting at the kitchen table, resting his forehead on his hand. He looked terrible. His face was a sort of dirty greyish colour, he hadn't shaved, and his eyes were bloodshot. He looked as if he had been up all night. He was certainly wearing the same clothes he had been wearing last night. When Billy came in he just looked up and grunted, and then winced as if the grunt had hurt his face.

His mother didn't look much better. She was standing by the cooker in her dressing gown, her face pale and puffy round the eyes, as if she had been crying a while ago. Her lips were pressed tightly together. She looked straight at Billy for a moment, then looked away.

Billy sat down at the table next to his dad.

"That set's got to go back," said his dad. "Something wrong with it."

"I saw it on the pavement," said Billy.

"Yes, he can just come and put it in his van."

"What happened?" asked Billy.

"I don't know," said his father. "I don't know what happened, and if I did know I couldn't explain it. Don't want any more of it, that's all."

"3D?" said Billy.

His father took his head out of his hands and looked at Billy.

"Yeah," he said finally. "Something like that."

"He can take his set and disappear," said his mother. "And I don't want our old one back either. He might have done something to that too."

"It's when you let him get round you," said his dad. 'That's where the trouble starts."

"He had such a lovely smile, too," said his mother, her eyes far away, and Billy couldn't tell whether she was talking about Alfonso Bonzo or Robert Mitchum or his father. Then she pressed her lips together again. After a moment she said, "If you see that Italian again, you're not to talk to him, understand?"

"Yes," said Billy.

"Promise?"

"Yes," said Billy.

Billy was very early for school that morning. It was partly the unusually early breakfast, partly that he wanted to get out of the house and up the road before

Alfonso Bonzo came to collect his Milanese TV set. When he got to the school yard he was almost the only one there. Just Brett Palfrey and Tubby Gerrish over the far side of the yard; they always came at crack of dawn and practised shooting-in against the brick wall. Brett Paifrey was the school goalie, and Tubby Gerrish, who had actually slimmed down years ago, but still kept his name, was a lethal striker of the ball and hadn't missed a penalty for two years.

Billy watched them for a bit, sitting on the wall. Funny, the things people were obsessed with. A lot of people were keen on football, of course, so it never occurred to them what a mad thing it was to do, getting up early winter or summer to pound about on the yard stubbing your toes on a sphere of leather full of air. Everybody was mad in one way or another, when you came to think about it. So really they ought to let each other alone a bit more than they did.

He was doing quite well at not thinking about Alfonso Bonzo, but the two football nutters were beginning to wear a bit thin as a source of distraction. Billy needed something physical. He stood up on the wall and began to walk along it, swinging his feet out in wide arcs with each step.

It was too easy if you just walked straight. The wall was only about one and a half metres high; you could jump straight down without even jarring your knees if you did it right, and it was two bricks thick, so you hardly needed the skills of a tightrope walker to manage it. It was of course against the school rules to walk on the wall, but most people did it, now and then.

When he'd done two laps of wide-arc walking, Billy went on to the next stage, which was shutting eyes for one step, then opening them for the next three steps. After that came shutting eyes for two steps, then three.

This was quite difficult, and kids often fell off the wall trying to do it. It needed a great deal of confidence and concentration; you couldn't think about anything else when you were doing it, and that was just what Billy needed that morning.

He had just finished his first lap of two-steps-eyes-shut when he knew he was not alone. He didn't need to turn round. He knew who it was.

"Good morning, Billy Webb, I see you are a bright and early boy, you got a good idea there, because it's a lovely day for business, no?"

Billy looked down. Alfonso Bonzo was in his working clothes again. Green hat, monkey jacket, green and yellow trousers, smile like clean white pebbles on an empty beach.

"Not talking to you," said Billy, realizing as soon as he'd said it that it didn't make proper sense.

"Hey, how you like Alfonso's ace TV set?" said the Italian exchange student, ignoring Billy's scowl. "Best TV set ever, no? Press 3D, get a piece of the action, I bet you have one brilliant time with that!"

"That was a dirty trick, that was," said Billy. Alfonso's face fell. A sad misunderstood look came over his face.

"Alfonso didn't mean no harm, Billy Webb. Maybe Alfonso go a bit too far sometimes, but no harm meant. All Alfonso wants is make people happy, you know that!"

"Well you can go and make someone else happy now, we've had enough, all right?"

"Hey. Billy Webb. Don't be like that with Alfonso Bonzo I don't want to make other boys happy, I want to make you happy, Billy Webb, the ace swapping boy, Alfonso Bonzo's special boy for business!"

"Push off," said Billy. He felt mean saying it, but he knew he had to. If he could say it to Ginger Gahagan he could say it to Alfonso Bonzo

"Brave boy," said the Italian Exchange Student. His smile wasn't quite so sweet any more. "Where you get your courage, eh? Who gave you that?"

"No one," said Billy uneasily.

"Yes, OK, Alfonso understand, you got your pride, you are very much like me. But you and me, we know inside, capisci?"

A low drone that had been growing steadily in the distance grew to a coughing spluttering roar. Not at all a pleasant sound, but Billy felt very glad to hear it. It was the sound of Mrs Peasgood's throaty old Triumph motor bike, known to her and her pupils as Temperamental Ted. Alfonso didn't look too pleased to hear it, though he turned his brilliant smile full on her as she chugged in through the gate, dismounted, and lugged it up on to its stand with a mighty effort, just ten metres from the wall.

She didn't seem to have noticed either of them, which was not surprising. Controlling Temperamental Ted demanded a lot of attention, and when she'd parked him he always seemed to need a lot of soothing down; and then she had to divest herself of about a ton of motorbike gear and haul about a hundredweight of books and projects and visual aids out of the side panniers.

So Billy Webb was able to carry on his conversation undisturbed, though he felt oddly comforted that his teacher was not too far away.

"Listen to me, Billy Webb," said the Italian Exchange Student. "I got one more little swap for you, the last exchange of all. You want to know what it is? I tell you, this one I wouldn't offer to any old boy. This swap a really ace swap for brilliant swappers only. This swap just for you."

"What is it?" said Billy reluctantly. He realized it was dangerous even to ask, but he had to know.

"You for me, me for you," said the Italian Exchange Student.

Billy didn't understand.

"You for me, me for you what?" he said.

"My life for your life. You have my life, I have your life. You be me, go anywhere, do anything, make anything happen you like. I be you, nice teacher, nice mama, bacon sandwiches in the kitchen. Nice idea, no?"

"How long?"

Alfonso Bonzo smiled. A new smile. A smile like faint sweet violins on the far side of a lake at dusk. A very tempting smile.

"What you like, Billy Webb. A day, a week, a month, a year, for ever. Lendsies or keepsies. You're the boss, Billy Webb. You my special boy for business."

Billy was thinking very hard. A day as Alfonso Bonzo would be mind-bending, an unforgettable experience. And Alfonso had always kept his word before. But the 3D TV set had been a lot more than the Webb family had bargained for. And he didn't think he trusted Alfonso Bonzo any more; he had the feeling that all the other swaps had been leading up to this one, and that Alfonso Bonzo had keepsies in mind, no matter what Billy decided. And there was another thing too.

"Look," said Billy. "If we did that swap, I wouldn't be me any more. I'd be you.

"You catch on quick, Billy Webb."

Billy thought some more. Being Billy Webb was not the most marvellous thing in the world, but being Billy Webb was what he was all about. He suddenly realized that he was Billy Webb and nobody else, and that was worth having, and he wasn't going to swap being Billy Webb for anything.

"Sorry," he said. "No swap."

Alfonso Bonzo was still smiling, but something else had come into the smile, a sharp burning smell that prickled the back of Billy's throat.

"Hey, listen, you crazy or what?" said the Italian Exchange Student. "You be Alfonso Bonzo, you could have one brilliant time, live like a king! You want to live in this dump for the rest of your life?"

Billy had never thought of Splott Street as a dump before, but now he did think about it, he supposed that a lot of people would call it a dump. Well, what if it was? It was his dump, and he liked it there. And yes. Now he had his answer.

"You seem to fancy this dump all right," he said. "No swap. Push off, Alfonso."

Suddenly, amazingly, tears appeared in Alfonso's eyes and started rolling down his cheeks.

"Please, Billy Webb. Just for an hour, just for a minute, let me be you, have a mama, papa, nice sister, warm kitchen, friends, be a real, Alfonso don't like being an exchange no more."

Billy had a sudden flash of understanding.

"Were you someone else before you were Alfonso Bonzo?" he said. "Someone like me?"

"Just for ten seconds, lendsies, I swear you!"

"No," said Billy. "I couldn't risk it."

The tears vanished off Alfonso's face as if they had never been there, and the Italian Exchange Student glared up at Billy Webb with a look of misery and hatred so intense that Billy would remember it for the rest of his life. Then, as suddenly as it appeared, the terrible look was gone, and the smile was back.

"OK, Billy Webb. No hard feelings. We did some nice business, you and me, you one very good boy for swaps, Alfonso Bonzo don't forget you. I go now. You don't see Alfonso Bonzo no more. Maybe you be sorry, maybe not."

"Won't be sorry," said Billy Webb. That seemed so harsh a thing to say that he added, "Spose I'll sort of, you know, miss you in a way."

"Arrivederci, Billy Webb! I go, I don't come back!" The Italian Exchange Student turned and walked away up Splott Street, his embroidered jacket flapping in the breeze.

"Billy Webb!" said Mrs Peasgood. "What are you doing on that wall? Get down now!"

"Just going to, Miss," said Billy. He wanted to watch Alfonso Bonzo all the way to the corner.

"Now please, Billy."

"Just going to, Miss."

At the corner, Alfonso Bonzo turned and waved. "Hey, Billy Webb!" His melodious voice floated down Splott Street. "Hey! Remember Alfonso Bonzo! Good luck! Break a leg, no?"

"Billy Webb," said Mrs Peasgood sharply, "get down this second!"

Billy wheeled round quickly, stumbled, and fell off the wall. He landed awkwardly, breaking his leg in two places.

Publisher's Note

Just before this book went to the printers, we received the following letter from Italy. We like to feel we are an honest bunch at Scholastic, so we decided to print it so that you can make up your own mind.

Letter from Alfonso Bonzo

This book is terrible. Who is this Davies who tells these lies about Alfonso Bonzo? He got one big problem with his brains: they don't work so good. If he ever meet me, he's one lucky man, because I exchange his brains for him, no charge. OK, OK, so some of the things he say are true. Where's the harm? Who suffers? Listen, you read this story, and I think you say, "Hey! I wish I could meet Alfonso Bonzo!" And maybe, one day, you will. Maybe you find me standing on your doorstep. Then you will have one brilliant time. Now. What are we going to do about this terrible book? I tell you. You read it, you don't like it, no problem. Pack it up and send it to me, and I exchange it for you. OK?

Alfonso Bonzo
(Italian Exchange Student)
Poste Restante